THE HOTEL LIFE

JAVIER MONTES

Translated from the Spanish by
Ollie Brock with Lorna Scott Fox

HB Hispabooks
Publishing

Hispabooks Publishing, S. L.
Madrid, Spain
www.hispabooks.com

Originally published in Spain as *La vida de hotel* by Anagrama, 2012
First published in English by Hispabooks, 2013
English translation copyright © by Ollie Brock with Lorna Scott Fox
Design and Photography © simonpates - www.patesy.com

A CIP record for this book is available from the British Library

ISBN 978-84-940948-6-6 (trade paperback)
ISBN 978-84-940948-7-3 (ebook)
Legal Deposit: M-30819-2013

For Vicente Molina Foix

What terrible rest! What a multitude of different kinds of serpents! What a terrifying place! What a wretched inn! If it is hard ... to spend one night in a bad inn, what do you think that sad soul will feel at being in this kind of inn forever, without end?

TERESA OF ÁVILA,
The Way of Perfection, Chapter 40, 9

I've brought just a light suitcase. I could easily have taken more, heavier bags, though, because the journey was a short one. Eight blocks—or zero point six two miles, according to the printed taxi receipt. It took me twenty minutes because of the traffic. No one said goodbye to me or closed the front door behind me; no one came with me, let alone followed me. But they were waiting for me when I arrived, with the room I was about to spend the night in reserved under my name.

I live so close to the hotel that it would have been quicker to walk. If I hailed a cab, it was only so that I would start the trip off on the right foot. It was still a trip, even if it was a short one, and I wanted to take it seriously from the outset. I have always taken my work and my trips seriously; in the end, they're more or less the same thing.

Or perhaps it was the exact opposite, and what mattered was knowing how to play, too, when the time is right for it. I've spent half my life going from one hotel to the next, but before now I had never slept in one in my own city. That's why, when they called from the newspaper to suggest I review the Imperial, I ended up agreeing to do it. I think we were all surprised that I did.

"They've finished remodeling it, they sent the brochure the other day."

At first I refused. They know I never write about new hotels.

"But this one isn't new. It's the same old Imperial. They've just given it a face-lift."

I don't like new hotels—the smell of paint, the piped-in music. And I don't trust refurbished ones. When they get a face-lift, they lose the character that stands for common sense and even sentiment—or at least for a good memory—in the old ones. I'm not sure I'm the sentimental type, but I do have a good memory. I'm starting to see that beyond a certain age, the two things blend into one, and that's almost certainly why I prefer hotels that know how to remember.

It's been a long time now since I settled my deal with the paper and gave them my conditions. I choose the hotel of the week. They pay. Expensive or cheap, near or far, big names or hidden gems, usually one night but sometimes two. No scrimping (they scrimp enough on my pay as it is) and no pitching hotels to me. I don't accept invitations in return for reviews.

And no, not even for a bad review, as I once had to explain over the phone to a PR rep who was either new or very clever.

Everyone in our little world knows that, but even so, a lot of invitations arrive for me at the office (I've forbidden them from giving out my details). They send them in the hope that one will slip through, I suppose, in case the day comes when I turn soft and agree to go and they spoil me and set me up in a nice, big room and I fill a page with glowing praise that they can frame and hang up in reception or post on their website, something that will bring the guests and their money flowing in—and that, even if it doesn't bring them in or they don't need it, will afford them things that are sometimes worth as much as money, or more: a seal of approval from the profession, the warmth of gratified vanity, the certainty that they are treading the righteous path of the hotelier.

Because it's true my column continues to be a big success. And even though they don't often tell me as much at the paper, so that it won't go to my head, I know that hotels, airlines, and travel agencies are tripping over themselves to get a half-page ad in "The Hotel Life". That's a relative sort of success, obviously, as is any success on the printed page. Every so often, someone encourages me to start a blog collecting together all my reviews. Even the people at the paper let it slip sometimes. OK, so we might be scuppering ourselves here, they'll say, but if you start a blog and put ads on up and find yourself a sponsor, you'll rake it in.

Personally, I'm not convinced.

"Anyway, you live right around the corner, don't you? You'd just have to go over there for a few hours one evening to see what they've done with the place."

Again I said no. Another thing they know is that I don't write about hotels I haven't slept in. It would be like reviewing a restaurant entirely on the strength of the smell of the food being brought out (of course my neighboring columnist, the food critic I share the page with, sometimes writes his "Table Talk" reviews that way: as I sit down at the table, I can tell from the smell alone exactly what they're cooking up in the kitchen, he told me on an occasion we ran into each other at one of those abysmal office parties that I stopped going to a long time ago. I didn't like the guy, and I suppose it was mutual).

"Well, don't let that stop you. You could always go and spend the night there."

It may have been a joke, but I took it seriously. Sleeping in a hotel room where I could look out the windows and practically see those of my own empty apartment and bedroom—I wasn't averse to the idea, and maybe for one night the novelty of it would do me good. I've gotten tired over the years, and I've spent a lot of those years in the same profession. It's the one I chose, true. And one that I do reasonably well, I think—perhaps better than anyone else, going by what the odd reader will tell me in an email, or even in an old-fashioned, signed-and-sealed, pen-and-ink letter, also forwarded to me from the paper.

The letters are open when they arrive. Apparently, it's for security reasons; indeed, the word *Security* is ostentatiously stamped in blue on the middle of the torn envelope. They're overdoing it a bit, I'd say; I can be harsh sometimes, but I don't quite deserve a letter bomb. All the same, it's good that they open them, and even that they read them—if it's true that they do read them—because that way the editors will know that I've still got my readers.

On the other hand, there's nothing so impressive about doing better than anyone else at a job in which there's almost no competition. There aren't very many of us hotel critics left, at least not in the newspapers. The internet is another story: everyone wants to post their opinions, recount the smallest details of their little escapades and even write things that aspire to the status of reviews (I think some of them are stealing my adjectives). That's no bad thing, I suppose. The reviews, on the other hand, are—they are almost always badly conceived, badly thought out, badly written, by bad people. Or strange people, at least; I like my work, but I wouldn't do it for free.

In the end, I gave in. Presumably, that's what the staff at the Imperial were hoping I would do when they tried their luck. They were delighted at the paper; they must have some advertising deal going. As always, they made the reservation under my name. Under my real name, that is—as is also always the case—and not the pseudonym I use for my column. The name on my ID card will throw the sharpest manager or receptionist off the scent and allow me to be just another hotel guest. And that's why I haven't let them put a picture of me next to my byline and why I never go to conferences or meetings with other critics. It's no sacrifice; from what I remember, the critics are as boring as their reviews. Being incognito makes my work easier and—why deny it?—more fun. It gives it a flavor of undercover espionage, makes me feel like a double agent. Or a double-double agent, because nobody is ever who they say they are in hotels, and everyone will take advantage of their stay, albeit unknowingly, to play detective.

After so many years of only using it to check in, my real name has come to seem more false to me than the false one; there aren't many who know it, apart from the people at the paper, and fewer still—perhaps none at all, to tell the truth—who use it.

At exactly midday, just as I waved the cab down, it started to rain. I had neither coat nor umbrella. I must have been the only one not expecting it, because within a minute the storm traffic had congealed on the street. I didn't mind. Actually, I would have been grateful if the journey had been even longer, even though I was paying and not the paper (I'm scrupulous on that point).

These days, the only kind of dashing around I do is in a taxi; it's the only kind I still believe in. I never even finished the hundred-yard dash of getting my degree, and I'd stopped feeling I was taking part in the race of life at all some time ago. I'd say I got off to a pretty good start. But then I lost sight of the other runners: the ones we're so aware of early on, in our twenties or at thirty, when we glance out the corner of our eye at those who are just behind us and trying to catch up (or so we think), when we calculate the distance the leaders have on us, conserve our energy, and plan shortcuts for the final sprint.

But there are no sprints that are worthwhile, I don't think, much less the final one. In truth, I stopped running a long time ago. Running's not worth it. We can walk at the speed that suits our feet best, and we'll still get to where we were going. Or we can just stay still; lately I've had the impression that it's things that move, not us. We just have to sit and wait—things don't fail, because nothing ever fails and everything always happens.

Everything was happening (and in its rightful order) outside the taxi's windows, at least: the utterly familiar streets, the doorways in single file, the treacherous flash of light as we turned a certain corner. Even while we were stuck in that traffic, everything kept passing by, as in the black and white taxis in old gangster movies, where the interior of the car was solid and still enough that a person could live in it forever, despite the mock hurricane of shaking that the strongest runners on the set were whipping up outside. And the actors would sit in front of the backdrop where dripping streetlamps and blurry sidewalks and pedestrians' ancient shadows were projected. Luckily for us, at night they always drove with the lights on inside the car. And it wasn't difficult to spot the trick they were using for the scenery in those movies. They were still so sure of themselves back then, perhaps they let it be obvious on purpose. The driver would spin the wheel without any turn registering in the background, or the background would just vibrate and shake and let shafts of light cut across it behind the outline of the windows. As though the man in charge of the special effects had simply gotten tired of pretending.

A similar thing happened in the cartoons that preceded the grown-up movies when we were children: the jabbering bear or the cat with the hat would run and run and run. And behind them, at great speed, a repeating sequence of trees and buildings flew past. It was done to save money—that way a single background drawing was enough for each character, fleeing in his cloud of dust. There was no need for anyone or anything to ever actually move in those fast-paced scenes. As a boy, I quickly discovered this looping technique; even before I could explain it, I was an expert at sniffing it out.

It occurred to me on the way to the hotel that I was running away in that unnecessary taxi. Or playing at running away, like the hammy policemen and gangsters. Because unless it's to try and give someone the slip, nobody gets into a car, without any luggage, only to check into a hotel ten blocks away. And if he does and someone really is following him, he'll look suspicious. It makes it seem like the person is trying to cover his tracks, just as they did—and do to this day—in old movies.

But nobody was about to follow me or shout "Follow that cab!" The driver wasn't even surprised at how short a ride it was to the hotel—in that car that itself felt like a hotel room where a person could stop for the night and imagine he was hiding from his pursuers.

It's all made up, of course. If it weren't for the updates I send the paper from hotels, I'd have been lost to everyone some time ago.

Twenty past twelve on a dull Tuesday afternoon in October: the bored doorman didn't open the door of the taxi for me, nor did he take my bag, but he did accompany me with an immense umbrella to the revolving door. Given the grandiose canopy we were

16

walking under, it was more ornamental than anything else; at most, it worked as a baton that set the tone for the rest of the hotel.

The two receptionists in the deserted lobby were bored as well; in fact, the whole hotel seemed to be bored in that unhappy hour of hotel lobbies, when no one of sound body or sound mind is in their room, when it's too late to check out, and too early to check in, and the tide of guests past and guests to come is stilled.

From close up, the receptionists looked very young and not very pleased to see me. Maybe the last thing they ever expected from that job was to find themselves having to check in a guest. The two of them, in perfect synchronization, riveted their eyes to the reservations screen. At their age, disdain and discomfort are hard to tell apart.

I hadn't been into the Imperial since I was a child. I've passed any number of times by the hotel's facade, which is as pompous as its name, and I've seen its two corner turrets from many a balcony. They still look new, but it's more than a hundred years now that they've been marking the location of the business district and helping to orient the outsider who looks on the city from a distance (and knows where to look). They were built as beacons of patriotic cosmopolitanism, and they looked irredeemably rancid from the start. Like the hotel itself—which had had its bullfighting appreciation meetings, its provincial casino air, and a lot of foot traffic at cocktail hour, but where no one ever seemed to spend the night.

The deathly silence of the lobby was in fact made up of many sounds: glasses clinking somewhere far off, the gallop of vacuum cleaners on the other side of the world. And, naturally, the sinuous, tenuous stream of piped-in techno music. It slithered between the legs of the furniture before coiling around your ankles and then going in one ear and out the other. It went with the new designer décor, which was splashed so prominently over the brochures sent on from the newspaper that I still can't even tell if I liked it. And I'm sure I'll never know, because that's the idea with these things: it's never supposed to matter much, really, whether you can tell or not.

I hear the previous owners sold the whole thing for next to nothing. Even so, the new owners obviously struggled to fund the remodeling. In the leaflets I had read, clichés of the genre abounded: this was a refuge for the wizened nomad, an operations hub for the international jet-setter. All so much superhero jargon that boils down to a few showy lamps that don't give off much light. Although they do give off enough to tell that the armchairs and carpets in the lobby will be less pleasant to the touch than they are to look at. The bell jars of wax flowers that I remembered dimly—no, not dimly: as vividly as a nightmare within a vague, blurred recollection—are gone. But they've held back on the real flowers, and in vain do they squirt their air freshener—even now, in the middle of the day, the ghost of bullfight-afternoon cigars still hangs.

And the ghosts of the bulls, too, because there is something that has been left over from before: on the wall behind the counter, as though for a joke, hang the stuffed heads of those that have seen fiercer days. A *Sobrero*, an *Embajador* and a *Navegante*, gazing now dumbfounded over everything below them. For a moment, I thought I recognized their faces. Or that their glass eyes twinkled as they recognized me. I saw myself, faintly, as a child: holding someone's hand and surrounded by adults who were talking without knowing how to take leave of one another, looking up at those same giant heads in the lobby, their tongues just barely sticking out of the second-rate stuffing. I don't know if it's a made-up memory or if I really did feel back then, as I did a moment ago, the same twinge of solidarity.

Another hotel acting as a sort of a mock-up or mascot for the whole country, a dollhouse and scale version of a real home that has the bad taste to display it in the parlor, or else leaves it to gather dust in the loft. The new Imperial has diluted its stale, stereotypical character, taken great pains to smooth out a few rough edges here and add in some new ones there, and finally scraped together a semblance of luxury held together with string. It still displays an erratic sort of sense in enjoying it.

And in proffering it. The receptionists' whispering and typing was becoming endless. I thought about taking out this little notebook, which rarely fails as a last resort—taking notes always gets the staff's attention. At long last, the machine spat out the magnetic key card for my room. They made no sign of calling anyone to take my bag, and I could swear the two of them handed me the key card together. But that must have been because of their disconcerting double smile.

The hallway on my floor was deserted and silent, as though it were five o'clock in the morning. Or, in fact, as though it were the exact time that it was, since there can be a lot of noise in a hotel at five o'clock in the morning. Not an employee or guest in sight. The only thing you could almost hear was the smell of new carpets thickening the air. I found my door and spent some time trying to discover the right way to put the magnetic card into the slot near the handle. Finally, a little light blinked red before turning green. The door groaned and then, without me pushing it, reluctantly opened an inch. Behind it there was a shadowy space: one of those hotel-room airlocks that serves as a no-man's-land and offers the luxury of a few square feet of space with no furniture and no name and no function other than to separate the room from the noise of the hallway, at least in theory.

To my left, the door to the bedroom, open just a crack, allowed in enough light to see the bathroom wide open in front of me. A glinting faucet dripped in the darkness. Before I had closed the door to the hallway, I heard a voice inside the room. For a moment I was paralyzed like a burglar caught in the act—an instinct I didn't know I had and which in any case was misplaced. To my left, something moved in the little entryway's full-length mirror. In it I could see the inside of the room that was obscured by the cracked door. There was the reflection of a double bed with a beige bedspread, which matched the gray light coming in through a window I couldn't see.

Sitting on the edge of the bed, near the head of it, was a girl. Attractive, despite some ill-advised makeup. She looked very young to me. She was wearing only a bra and panties. Her hair and skin were the same color as the bedspread. She had her hands in her lap and was gazing down at them with a bored expression. She puffed out her cheeks a little, tapped her feet on the carpet, sighed scornfully; she was going out of her way to signal her boredom, like the child who isn't really bored.

Out of the corner of her eye, she was following something that was going on at the end of the bed not reflected in the mirror. She wasn't alone. The bed springs creaked without her moving, and someone—a man, clearly—panted once, twice, three times.

I didn't know whether to go back out into the hall or come all the way in and demand an explanation. They couldn't see me, so I took another step forward, still watching the mirror. The girl's reflection passed out of the frame. Kneeling on the bedspread at the other end of the bed, with his back to the headboard and the girl, was a naked boy. A bit younger than the girl, much darker skin. I couldn't see his face because he was hanging his head and looking apologetically at his chest; what I could see was his tense forehead, the strain of his furrowed brow. He continued breathing like one preparing for some great exertion, and he ran his hand over his chest with an unfeeling, robotic sort of gesture. Then the girl spoke.

"Why don't you touch yourself?"

The boy gave a start and looked at her as if he had forgotten she was there.

"OK, OK."

He concentrated on his hand again and let it slip slowly over his stomach down to his belly button. He seemed unconvinced, but he moved it all the way down to his limp penis, which he shook a few times like a rattle. He shuddered suddenly, tensing his shoulders.

"Fuck, it's cold in here."

"Mm-hmm."

The girl's "Mm-hmm" was deeply resigned, as though they had performed this exchange a thousand times; as though she had spent her life in that room, in her underwear, listening to people complain of the cold. I assumed she was arching her eyebrows and nodding with an affectation of sardonic solemnity, but to know for sure, I would have had to look away from the boy's face. She must have liked the air of a woman of the world that her "Mm-hmm" lent her, because she repeated it.

"Mm-hmm."

He started to pant again and resumed his task, in vain. The next time he let out a groan, the girl joined him in it.

"OK, what's up?"

"I don't know, man, why don't you help me?"

"Come on, you know we've talked about this. No, I'm not going to, you have to do it yourself. Then we fuck."

"But I can't get hard."

"So watch the movie."

The girl suddenly adopted the tone of an older sister.

"One second, hold on, I'll turn the volume up."

I could hear her looking for something next to the bed, things falling onto the carpet. I didn't dare change position in order to turn and look at her. I started to get scared they would see me. The idea of going into the room, looking shocked, and claiming what was rightfully mine had disappeared of its own accord. I ought to have gone down to reception. To tell the truth, I don't know if I stayed for fear of making noise as I went out or because I wanted to see and know more. It seemed I could get away with waiting a little longer; if the boy or the girl got up, I would have time to go out into the hallway and close the door before they saw me.

"Great, now I can't find the remote."

The boy said nothing. He was busy massaging his genitals with both hands. He did it carelessly—in a strangely clumsy way, as though he had never had to touch them before. Suddenly, a chorus of moans over some ludicrous music burst into the silence: the unmistakable soundtrack of a porn movie.

"Oh. There. There. Oh."

I realized I was smiling as I stood there in the entryway. A companionless smile is always a false one. I probably wanted to lighten my mood, or even the mood of the entire scenario—given the stimuli on offer, I wasn't surprised that the boy was having trouble getting an erection.

"Turn that down, the whole hotel's gonna hear it."

"OK, OK, wait a sec."

The moans and the music cut out just as a gruff, unconvincing voice was joining the ensemble.

"Yeah. Uh-huh. Uh-huh. Yeah."

The boy was looking at the screen. He must have been right next to the door to the entryway, and for a moment, I thought he could see me through the wood; my heart thumped, and I felt my throat tighten. But

23

no—what the boy was looking at through the crack was his own image in the mirror. Apparently, that worked better than the mechanical panting from the movie. His reluctant penis began to show signs of life. He turned a little to face his reflection full on. This boy, I thought at that point, is seeing exactly the same thing as me and is being turned on by exactly the same thing that I'm looking at without being turned on: his own image cast back at him by this mirror in the middle of this dark, little room. It was the image that my own reflection—the wrinkled back of my sports jacket—would replace if I were to take another step forward.

In the shadows of that little entryway that was neither hallway nor bedroom, standing a few feet from the mirror, I almost felt I was in the boy's presence. The rectangle of light that framed his body blocked my way like a brick wall: I couldn't go into the bedroom without pushing the slightly-open door and interrupting the scene inside, and I couldn't go back out into the hall without putting myself between the boy and his double. After a few seemingly endless moments—I scarcely dared breathe—I heard the dripping of the bathroom faucet again, the strap of my bag dug into my shoulder a little more, and I knew that I was going to get tired of standing. Perhaps a space of even more senseless boredom was going to open up in the midst of my foolish anxiety. There was the darkened room, the awful paralysis of nightmares or children's games; more than anything, I noticed that the knot in my throat had been slowly tightening its grip and would soon resemble a sort of black, infantile panic.

The boy was now masturbating openly. For a second or two, I found myself watching everything without really seeing anything, and he and I gave the same start when we suddenly heard the voice of another man in the bedroom.

"No, no, this is good. Don't turn around, keep looking over here."

There was someone else in the room. The boy turned around again, looking away from the mirror. I started breathing again at this point (and realized I had gone some time without remembering to do so).

"That's better. You're right, it is cold. You keep going, I'll shut the door."

And maybe I shouldn't have started breathing again, because the new air in my lungs made me let my guard down. Panic gripped me harder and shot straight to my head—I felt its hands squeeze my shoulders, stroke my neck, and push into the corners of my eyes before slapping me silently. It had understood what those words meant before I did. Now the owner of the voice would come up to the entryway door and find me and it would be terrible. I pressed my back to the wall. There was nothing in the mirror now. On the other side of the cracked door, I heard footsteps approaching on the carpet—of course, I may have imagined them, or felt them in the soles of my feet or somewhere in the deepest reaches of my hearing, because I think that carpet would have smothered the sound of an entire army marching over it. I saw myself from outside my body—or from above it, to be precise—and it felt as though I had a whole eternity to calculate what was going to happen (and what wasn't going to happen). There were many variations of my imagined confrontation with the owner of the voice: angry—"What are you *doing* here!"; surprised—"What are *you* doing here?"; ominously cruel and ironically amused—"Well, well. Look who we have here …"; or worst of all, there was the possibility of absurd astonishment from both parties—"Oh—!"

It is only now, as I write all this down, that I realize the one thing that didn't occur to me was that the room was mine, after all, and that the law, as they say, was on my side. Of course it was, there are no two ways about it; and yet, at that moment, the no-man's-land of that little entryway was beyond the reach of almost everything, and certainly beyond the reach of the law.

Then the door closed. Someone pushed it from the inside, and it closed just like that. I didn't see a thing: not a hand, not so much as a shadow. I felt a sense of relief mixed with hints of a sort of bewildered disappointment. On the other side, the footsteps of the voice's owner withdrew. I could still hear him.

"There really was a draft."

I heard nothing more—neither the voice of the boy or the girl, nor the porn soundtrack. I breathed deeply again, and just then, my accumulated panic overflowed. For another endless second, I felt my feet welded to the floor. I would never be able to quit the limbo of that cramped, little entryway—which was terribly dark, more of a purgatory, really—now that the mirror was no more than a black surface. Then, suddenly, a few miraculous strides and I was back outside the room again, closing the door very slowly. The hallway was still deserted.

Only then did I notice the red *Do not disturb* sign hanging from the handle. I even pretended to get upset with myself: Oh, sure, now you see it, I almost said aloud. My heart was returning to its normal rhythm, and I felt the euphoria that had always followed in the wake of my rather modest troublemaking when I was a child. And now I realize that I was still thinking from a child's point of view: I was OK, I was in one piece, I was alive, safe and sound. *They*—the bad guys, the grown-ups—hadn't caught me.

At last, the adult took his rightful place again, rolled up his sleeves, and banished to some dark corner the brave, faint-hearted child who had taken the reins for a moment. After all, I thought, I had surely not done or seen anything wrong. An odd scene, true. Difficult to understand. Strange.

I didn't feel up to getting in the elevator, so I looked for the emergency stairs. No carpet, air freshener, or piped-in music. It was cold, and my footsteps rang out over the dull hum of muffled machinery at the bottom of the bottomless stairwell.

"No, not strange—really strange."

I think I said that out loud as I continued down the stairs. I took them two at a time, until I got to the basement and had to come back up them one by one.

Yes, that's right, and would I please excuse them. The receptionists smiled at me—just a little, but both of them at once. It's a rough day, they said. They looked around as though the lobby were heaving with complaining guests, as though we, or they, were still in the old hotel, at peak hours on the day of the season's biggest bullfight. In addition to cards for specific rooms, the machine can also create master cards that open all the doors. Like old housekeepers' skeleton keys, they told me.

I suppose they thought that nostalgia for a more handcrafted world was reassuring. It wasn't, but I didn't have time to look alarmed; they've promised me that only authorized personnel use those cards. I can rest easy, the privacy of the rooms is absolute. The operating system was unoperative due to a routine reconfiguration. This has never happened before and they don't expect it will ever happen again.

Their lack of surprise surprised me. They didn't exchange a single look of mutual reproach or shared disdain throughout the whole conversation. Nor did they say anything else about it, and I didn't go into any awkward details. The three of us just stood there in silence—the scene from my initial check-in was replaying itself identically. As though I were arriving at the hotel again, once again for the first time.

It didn't last long; in a strict division of labor, they each went to opposite ends of the counter. The one on the right operated the card machine. "Operate" may be an overstatement; he pressed the same button as before and then stood there staring at it. And the one on the left had only to pick up the telephone for a bellhop— also short on smiles—to materialize at my side. He'll accompany you to your room, one of them told me. I don't remember which. Or perhaps neither of them said it, and it was just understood.

"It's 206, not 207."

They didn't apologize again. I think they considered the extravagant gesture of summoning a bellhop to be contrition enough.

206 is identical to the room next door, except that now the bedroom is to the right of the entryway. The beige bedspread; the gray privacy curtains that make what's left of the day—already limping to a close outside— even grayer. As it starts to rain again, it could be any time of day: seven in the morning or in the evening. And this could be almost any place, too; seen from up here on the second floor, filtered by the blinds, the little strip of street through the windowpanes could be a nondescript street from any one of a thousand cities. A neutral setting, you could say, for the adventures of our protagonist.

It remains to be seen, of course, what those adventures are—if they occur at all, that is. And who their protagonist will be, since this isn't the first time I've felt like I'm a background character with no lines, hovering around the main action, out of frame.

As I followed the bellhop, I went past my neighbors' door. It looked innocent enough. Not a single sound disturbed the ethereal peace of the hallway. And I can't hear anything now, either. Only the partition wall separates the pillow on my bed from the one in the next room over, but it must be good and thick, because no pornographic pants or flesh-and-blood voices are coming through it. As though there were nobody on the other side, or perhaps nothing at all; as though the set, or the world, ended at this side of the dividing wall.

I confess that after the bellhop left without saying a word or waiting for a tip, I climbed onto the bed and put my ear to the wall. Then I did something I have only seen in movies: I took a glass from the bathroom—an identical glass and an identical bathroom to the ones I had glimpsed next door. I placed the rim against the wall and pressed my ear to the base. To little effect: just the gravelly breath of the plumbing over the hotel's heartbeat, which palpitated up from the depths of the boiler room.

Perhaps I had gotten it wrong and they don't really do it like that in the movies. Perhaps, for the trick to work, the glass has to have a little hole in the bottom. In another hotel, or at this same hotel in another time, it would have had one—for the water to drain out of after you'd used your toothbrush.

I felt ridiculous, and I sat down to write in this notebook, on this very low, extremely uncomfortable little table. There is no sign of a desk or a stationery set—international nomads have no need for them. Scanning back, I see that my notes are longer than I thought. I don't usually take many while I work, and I haven't brought a spare notebook; this one is already half filled, and I'm not sure whether I would prefer that everything fit in here, or if it would be better to run out of pages in the telling of everything that happens.

If anything does happen, that is. I'm hungry; I must have missed dinnertime. I've just eaten a small chocolate that was wrapped in silver paper and worth its weight in gold. The little fridge is as rancid as the peanuts inside it: a relic of the old hotel lurking behind the metal facing that keeps the minibar cool and brings it into line with the "cool" feel of the room. It has made me think of the photos I had seen in the elevator, above the control panel. The old lounges and dining rooms were oozing with saturated colors, decked out in all their pomp and in dubious circumstances: gathered curtains, toothpick holders, shellfish crackers. In one, complete with lurid yellow rice, larger-than-life local delicacies were laid out on wheat and grapevine stalks. The gums of the *maîtres d's* holding the suckling pig helped place it all somewhere in the seventies—more or less when I must have come to this hotel for the first time. If the memory isn't in fact borrowed from another hotel or concocted altogether.

These photos have also survived the refurbishment, but they'll take them down as soon as there's money to outfit the elevator in the same metal facing as the minibar. They're odd, these reservoirs of time that sometimes pool up. Care must be taken, as I know only too well, not to venture too far into these lakes grown out of wasted hours; just like in the comics, shark fins will sometimes appear, and we can find ourselves being swallowed up.

Across from the bed, next to the door into the entryway, there is an immense television, quite flat. (Even I, who don't have a clue about these things, know that there are much flatter ones. But that's no one's fault—there's always going to be a flatter one on the market.) It, too, must be identical to the one in the other room. And the same mirror shows me my reflection from the entryway, through the door that I prefer to leave wide open for now. It looks as though it opens onto a neighboring room, where my exact double is living his hotel life.

I turned on the television, laid down on the bed, and flicked through the stations until I arrived at the inevitable porn channel. For ten seconds, a few women struck acrobatic poses and threw up a chorus of moans. Then the screen went dark, and some green lettering glowed mournfully: *This is a pay per view station. For more information, please contact reception.*

That's what my neighbors had done, of course: pay to view. But this small flicker of detective-like success is too little, too late. It's doubtless the first and last part of this adventure that doesn't look like it's going to go anywhere. I thought about calling reception and paying to watch what they're watching, or perhaps will watch, or at any rate have watched in room 206. But I was put off by the certainty of sensing that double smile, which really would be conspiratorial this time, coming down the line from the two receptionists.

And there is one thing I absolutely refuse to do, and that is to stake myself out in the hallway. It could take hours, and I hate waiting hours for things that aren't scheduled to happen at any particular time and may never happen at all. It's possible no one would go into or come out of the room next door until noon tomorrow at the earliest. I drank a whiskey, neat, out of my novice-spy glass—I, who never drink at this time of day. It was a bad idea and it went down badly; now I can feel the beginnings of a headache that an aspirin alone won't take care of. Perhaps my experiment is working—I feel, or perhaps I find myself obliged to feel, an imitation of that nostalgia for country, city, and home that the man who has traveled thousands of miles and is not sure he will return feels. And now what? Now, nothing: I've said it loud and clear and I'm writing it down here to see if I can make the disappointment I've felt since I came into this room just a little bit more ridiculous.

If nothing else, I will do my professional duty. I will conduct an inspection of closets, examine all complimentary soaps and shampoos. Perhaps I'll get up, walk around the hotel a bit, take a few notes that might be useful—before I fill this notebook with rather more useless notes like these. I'd decided not to bring any books, and if I stay in the room, I'll run the risk of finding myself reading the brochures on the bedside table: guided tours of the city; laundry service; a menu of sheets in case I want to choose the color or even the scent of the ones I will sleep on. Apparently, offering this contrivance of company to those who travel light and alone is in vogue.

The Hotel Life

Expert relaunch, or a patch-up bursting at the seams? This week, our critic investigates the new look of an ageing classic. Spend a night with him in the old Imperial Hotel and see if it is truly rejuvenated.

THE BULL BY THE HORNS

Or, "The Roof Over Your Head". I'll admit that I was about to use that title for this review of the (nearly) brand-new remodeling of the good old Imperial.

And that's because I'll start with its rooftop deck, which, following the overhaul, is only open to guests during the day, and at night to customers of the outdoor bar they'll set up there in the summer. It's the centerpiece of the new facilities. At least, that's what they're calling it. As you know, I research these flimsy reviews as a plain-clothes guest, and I must say that, as of now, it isn't an easy place to visit.

But I insisted. And I'm afraid it wasn't just so I could recount the experience to you here. I have a weakness for rooftop decks. As a child, I used to love going up to the one on our building. It wasn't all that high, but the world, or the city, or at least the courtyards on our block (the three came to more or less the same thing), when seen from above like that, promised adventure. Thick foliage bloomed and garage roofs sprouted here and there, all of it invisible from sidewalk level. And the windows on the other side of the road suddenly seemed to conceal a gold mine of youthful intrigue.

I've said it a thousand times in this column, and you'll have to forgive me for saying it again: to sleep in a hotel is to return to one's childhood. To that time when the bedding changed itself and a comforting, turned-down sheet kept guard over the four corners of the bed during the night. Climbing out onto a rooftop also reawakens the intrepid, domestic explorers we once were.

The one at the Imperial could not be visited. Which was a shame because it's sure to be one of the city's loveliest (and there's no such thing as an ugly rooftop deck, so that's saying something). It has its hidden little corners, its views of downtown and of the mountains in the distance—all in the shadow of the two towers on the facade, which from close up have an air of ruins of long-forgotten civilizations about them.

Not just anybody could go up on the roof of the building I grew up in, either. My mother had wrangled a contraband set of keys from the doorman. Sometimes, in early summer, at siesta time, when the smell of respectable stews hung in the air on the landings and not a whisper was to be heard behind any door, she would go up to sunbathe. She wore a swimsuit under her brightly colored dressing gown and would take a book with her that would come back down unopened.

Sometimes she would let me go with her. Now, I'm surprised to think of it, because silence was mandatory, and running and shouting were not allowed up there. For one hour, the two of us would become thieves, partners in a crime committed in broad daylight, walking on tiptoe across the searing roof at four in the afternoon.

As I say, it wasn't a particularly beautiful roof—there were no plants or awnings, no sheets hung out to dry. The rough floor tiles somehow both scorched the soles of your feet and made you shiver. In the middle, there was a white, windowless little hut. Out of the slats in its small door came the squeaking of gears, the grunt of machinery: the elevator pulleys stirring themselves as someone, deep down in the pit of the stairwell, went up to their apartment or down to street level in the middle of the siesta heat.

Sometimes a French neighbor of ours, younger than my mother, would already be there when we arrived. She seemed to exaggerate her accent in jest, and she didn't move except to dovetail one cigarette with another. She may or may not have sunbathed topless. And I may or may not have invented the memory of her perfect breasts. But in any case, she was different, and she seemed more attractive to me up there than the times I would see her down in the lobby, when, wearing her street clothes and a smile, she would make me feel like I was her co-conspirator, and all the blood would go to my head. I'll say it again: that roof was nothing out of this world. But for me, its rusty door did somehow open onto another world.

Somewhere you will find sheets on a rooftop, however, is at the new Imperial. They hang from recently erected trellises, forming canopies and covering the sofas—their plastic still on— that surround the bar in the middle. They might look better in the months to come, be flattered by the summer nights. But for now, the impression is pretty bleak.

It could be that the management know it, too, because getting up there was more complicated than getting ahold of the keys to the roof terrace of my boyhood. Only after a number of visits to reception, a flurry of phone calls, a lot of to-ing and fro-ing on the part of the staff, and the odd disconcerted look did I get them to open the glass door that leads to the roof. This was without any subtle exchanging of tips, I should point out. But let this be a warning to the unsuspecting guest: the views are worth the effort. But you will have to earn them.

This is no good, and they won't like it at the paper, either. They've grumbled lately when I've written things like this. You've got a very personal style, they'll say, but this is a review column. Childhood memories can give a piece some flavor, but we can't have them taking up the whole page.

And these were memories I hadn't revisited in awhile; I'm sure that if I hadn't gone up to the roof, they would have remained in the deepest basement of my mind for a very long time. I've come to the hotel bar to write and to warm up. I can't write at the tiny table in my room, and the idea of going back to sharing a wall with my now silent neighbors was making me nervous.

There's no point sitting on the roof with the way it's coming down out there. After all my insistences that they open it for me, the bellhop made a face when I only stayed up there for three minutes. And of those three, two were just to make him feel better and justify the panic that had descended on reception when I went down to say I wanted to see the roof.

41

"They haven't finished setting it up. In fact, it's still not officially open."

Luckily, the twin receptionists' shift was over. There was a girl there now, also very young. With her, at least I could read the irritation writ large on her face.

"It's not going to be very nice, with the way it's coming down out there."

And the truth is that it wasn't. But I was irritated by her irritability. There was still not a single guest to be seen in the lobby, and it didn't look to me as though the bellhop had anything better to do. The elevator control panel had a lock next to the button that took you to the roof. He turned the key in it in silence, and we didn't talk during the ride. Nor did I allow him to follow me with an umbrella on my little walk around the roof. The whole scene was suddenly seeming stupid enough as it was, without him playing the movie butler into the bargain. I told him to wait for me somewhere he could keep dry. And that didn't go down well, either—I think he was pleased that it was pouring down and that the whole thing was a disaster.

I walked over to the edge, more to get away from his eloquent poker face than out of any genuine curiosity. It smelled of turpentine and wet sawdust. The streetlights in the square came on right at that moment. They steamed orange in the rain. A hushed dusk, without ambition or intrigue, was falling over the withered horizon of rooftops and antennae. I couldn't quite see the windows of my empty apartment from up there as I had thought I would be able to. But I do think I was able to more or less make out my building's rooftop deck. I can't be sure;

things are very different when seen from that height and I have never, in twenty years of living in that building, thought to go up on the roof. From a distance, it didn't look very different from the building I grew up in, which in the end never quite delivered on the adventures and mysteries it promised.

Or perhaps it did, and I didn't know it.

I leaned out further so that I could see the facade of the hotel from above. Almost half my body was hanging over the edge. All the while, I could feel the bellhop's disapproving gaze boring into my back, and I would have loved him to think I was going to jump. Now that really would be a nuisance, for him and for the entire Imperial hierarchy—no establishment can survive the suicide of the critic reviewing it. And there could be no more personal review, of course; even my editors would have to admit that. The sort of farewell to my column that would really make a splash.

It wasn't difficult to locate the window of my room, three floors below—it's the only one in the entire hotel that's open. My neighbors must still be shut up inside their own. Through their window came the blue flickers of a television in the darkness.

Now I get the feeling our two rooms were the only ones showing any signs of life in the whole building. Or perhaps that's another of my made-up recollections. I know from experience that my memory is more selective than I think. The truth is, up there, I only had eyes for the furious blinking coming from my neighbors' room.

A breeze began to blow, freshening the smell of paint. I felt dizzy as I straightened up from the railing, like a shipwrecked man in reverse, standing on his ghost ship; I would have liked to wave my arms and call out to the umbrellas crossing the streets below, safe on their dry land. The bellhop came over, too, eventually, and gave me a fright that could have ended badly.

"I thought there was a fire."

We looked each other in the face for the first time. It was one of those cryptic comments that are easily decoded. I think he was regretting it even as he spoke. He was embarrassed by the sudden, involuntary intimacy that had sprung up between us, inexplicable and faintly repellent—we were sudden accomplices in who knows what. I wasn't able to do anything other than smile and go back to the elevator. Feverish with the smell of turpentine, and the cold, and altitude sickness.

"Jesus, the lobsters I have to eat just to bring home the bacon!"

I had made a tactical withdrawal to the reading room an hour ago when the hotel bar filled with fifty-somethings, their bellies spilling over their belts. They were roaring with laughter and slapping each other on the back. The room had been a funereal sight when it was empty, but this was worse. The waiters were overwhelmed by the sudden invasion. I closed my notebook and prepared to flee. But before I could turn around, as I stood at the bar, somebody pulled a prank that hadn't been tried on me since I was twelve: the sharp jab to the back of the right knee that makes the joint give way and the person nearly fall over if he's caught unawares. It's an odd sensation to lose one's footing suddenly. Not altogether unpleasant, but at that moment, I found it annoying.

"And the caviar, and the oysters too! How you doing, neighbor?"

Sure enough, it was my neighboring columnist, the restaurant critic. When I turned around, there he was in his wheelchair, laughing. And so I don't think the jab to the leg was, in fact, intentional; it was just the part of me most within his reach. Still, he seemed to be treating me with a greater degree of familiarity than really exists between us. Before today, I don't think we had met more than one or two times, at the newspaper's annual dinners. I suppose he reads me every week, as I do him, and that can, even if only very obliquely, make for a sort of fellow feeling.

I think he was a bit tipsy. Perhaps he always talks to people like that. Or perhaps he's always tipsy. Because now I remember that he had bellowed out his lobster line at the last newspaper dinner, too, as he took his seat at the table we were sharing (or as he pulled up to it, rather). And he was overfamiliar and droll throughout the meal, and he kept calling me "neighbor." It's odd, because he doesn't have the right physical appearance for the role: he jokes, but his eyes don't joke; in fact, they rarely blink. Of course, he drops that tone when he writes. In "Table Talk", he will often make it clear that, even as he ladles on the praise, the subjects of his reviews will still feel sick on reading them.

He explained to me that the invading army was a group of guests on a press junket at the hotel, as the owners wanted to present their new restaurant and that season's menus. The umpteenth example of the fact that everything comes round in the end—now that I don't go to a single one of these events, they end up coming to me. They had just come out, he said, of an immensely long post-prandial session in one of the dining rooms, with speeches, coffee, drinks, and cigars.

"They invited me because they know I'm preparing the second volume of *A Hundred Menus to Try Before You Die*. I imagine you've read the advance in the paper."

I hadn't, nor had I read volume one. But I do know that it's a huge hit, that there is no contemporary household or modern couple that doesn't have it on their shelves and follow it like the Bible, and that it must be going into its tenth edition by now. (Actually, it would be impossible not to know—they coo about it at the paper on a daily basis.) But I wasn't about to apologize; he has never remarked on a single word in any of my reviews. In fact, I doubt he's read any of them. As for his writing, what I like are the adjectives; I can't be absolutely certain he's using them ironically, but you have to admit that they're inspired. No one writing in the Spanish language has previously dared to pronounce a prawn "playful," or to chew on an "insolent little rump steak."

He laughed and slapped me on the knee before giving me a chance to reply. His eyes betrayed no doubt—not for a moment did he think I'd read it.

"Naturally, I'm going to include this place."

He used his arms to push himself up in his seat, and I found myself leaning down so that he could whisper something to me. Not exactly in my ear, but he was suddenly much closer to my height.

"Because this really was one of those menus you try just before you die."

He sat looking at me, waiting to see my reaction. I think he was ready to explode with devilish laughter at the slightest sign of complicity from me. But he's a quick man, and at the last moment he opted instead for stroking his small, white, Mephistophelian beard and laughing mostly to himself, shaking his shoulders more than necessary.

His goatee is pointy, but it doesn't make his features any sharper. I found his face even fleshier than I had remembered it, marbled with every hue from saffron to eggplant. The idea with the little beard, I suppose, is to dignify his face, give him an air of some sort of Falstaff of the flame grills. But it only does half the job, just as this man is only half served by his farmhand's figure; strong arms and big hands frame the solid belly of a *bon viveur*, but his thin legs and his small feet turned inward on the footrest cut the impression short. At the dinner with the paper, someone had asked him over dessert if it was difficult to visit restaurants incognito. He laughed and answered that we would be surprised how easy it is to slip under the radar in a wheelchair.

"You really think I'd be a food critic if it weren't for the chair?"

That day he really did guffaw, and every one of us at the table chimed in with him. In fact, I remember all of us feeling awkward and laughing nonstop all evening.

"You're also here for work, I take it."

His eyes grew steely again and belied the large smile that was forming a few inches below.

"Or is it for pleasure?"

It's not just his body, I thought; on his face, too, there are two halves that don't add up. You might even say they contradict or cancel each other out. At that moment, it seemed as though none of his jokes were innocent. Now I think it's more that he finds the very idea of innocence the best joke of them all.

Perhaps it's all a question of physiognomy—faces can be so disorienting. There are people who carry their features around as though they had won them in a raffle, people who gesticulate at random and never quite understand what their own gestures mean.

But I'm reminded again that we hardly know each other; perhaps he was just looking at me like that to build up the nonexistent sense of ease between us that he considers it so imperative to affect.

"Well, our work is a pleasure, isn't it?"

It wasn't much of a comeback on my part, but he celebrated it with the burst of laughter he had been holding in from before, and which again seemed inappropriate. Or all too appropriate, if what he was really laughing at was my attempt to dodge his real question with some arthritic old joke.

Now that I'm writing this, it seems absurd to have given so much thought to a formulaic conversation. But this man has a knack, when you're face to face with him, for making you think you're hiding something. Or even for making you remember that that's exactly what you're doing. If we ever did talk about these things (which we never will), perhaps we would agree on that. Almost everybody is hiding something, and we ought to feel especially suspicious of anyone who is convinced of not hiding a thing.

"You think? I'd say we work for the pleasure of others."

I laughed the strained laugh of our dinner companions from that other night.

"Or at least to facilitate it," he added, no longer laughing, although it was just then that his eyes smiled for the first time.

"So, yeah. I don't know how many stars you have to rack up before you can take a vacation, but I've got a lot of forks and a lot of seafood to get through this season. I've got bookings under my name all over the country the next six months, and I'm judging five different prizes. And I could yak on and on about all the talks I have to give. But actually, they don't count, because I always rehash the same one—I just garnish it a little differently each time, so to speak."

His boasting didn't surprise me. Nor did I think any of it was untrue. I had rid myself a long time ago of the adolescent notion that people only show off what they don't have. Vanity is independent of merit—that's the mystery of the thing. Sometimes the former exceeds the latter, true; but sometimes it simply comes standard, out of sheer compulsion or habit. It's not my style, but in cases like his, I admit I don't find it wholly objectionable. Anything is better than false modesty—and modesty is always false when it isn't superfluous.

What did surprise me, on the other hand, was that he had so many bookings under his name. Supposedly, it goes against the professional code of conduct. He must have seen it in my face.

"Well, I'll leave you to it. The hotel's PR rep is on her way over, you don't want her finding out who you are. I know you're a big believer in staying incognito."

I don't know *how* he knows. Gossip at the paper, maybe, although I understand he goes into the office even less than I do.

"I hope your minibar's good and stocked, because I've got nothing I can recommend to you for dinner. They've really taken to heart the idea that 'sauces are back.' Or maybe they just never knew they'd gone."

He maneuvered his chair with precision as he spoke. In a flash, he was already more than halfway to the other end of the bar. He turned back a little once more before disappearing.

"And good luck with your work. I don't think either of us would ever end up here for pleasure."

The guffaw he let out doubled as a greeting to the cluster of people that was heading toward him.

I went up to my room after having been run aground for an hour in the reading room, which was also deserted, and which had been reupholstered in coordinating shades of aquamarine. There were no stuffed bulls. What had survived, however, in a similarly comic vein, were the bell jars of wax flowers that I had missed in the lobby. In times past, they must have held solemn sway over the room.

The place was deserted, and there was not a single shelf, or book, or anything else in the room—except the sign at the door—that conjured the idea of reading. An ancient and vaguely familiar waiter came in a number of times to ask me what I wanted to drink. I could just hear the distant strains of the epicures lingering in the bar. Now and then, a chorus of laughter would play counterpoint to the immediately recognizable laugh of my page neighbor.

I can now admit to myself what I didn't want to put into words when I was downstairs. I stayed there in the reading room in the hope of catching sight of my other neighbors. From the armchair I was in, I enjoyed a commanding view of the elevators, through the large archway that formed the entrance to the reading room. At any moment, the boy or the girl or both of them might have appeared, either on their own or accompanied by the owner of the voice who had shut the door in my face without knowing it. Perhaps I would have followed them out into the street or to the dining room; perhaps I would have chanced a conversation with them, from one armchair to another. But the elevator doors didn't open once, and the hubbub from the bar was affecting my mood. I didn't care much, just then, if they were truly having a good time or if all the guffawing was false. I was envious: it sounded like quite the party.

The waiter kept incessantly changing untouched ashtrays. I've just realized, as I write, why he looked familiar. Nothing to do with childhood memories. He was one of the *maître d*'s from the old photographs in the elevator, now with a lighter moustache. Apparently, he too had survived the remodeling of the Imperial.

I barely made it around the awful horn of that awful hour. Every so often, I would stop writing, look up, and check the clock; the elevators and the clock hands would be exactly as I'd left them. In the end, a soggy feeling of despair soaked through my body. There is no traveler who doesn't carry it with him in his suitcase, and no hotel where it doesn't come free with the room. We're old acquaintances now, and I've had to confront the feeling on my own more than once. I prefer it that way, to tell the truth. There is only one melancholy worse than that of the solitary traveler: the double melancholy of traveling companions, each aware of how his own is made worse by the other's attempt to hide what he's feeling.

But I notice I'm feeling less brave today. Travel and all its private, asinine little dilemmas (how much shall we pay? where shall we eat? when should we sleep?) can degenerate into a creeping feeling of sadness, into that distinctive, identical desolation that lies in ambush in every room in every hotel in the world. Ten years ago it all felt less dangerous, more subject to objections, to bargaining; in those days, that hotel-room desperation was scarcely even a rustling noise behind the curtains or a claw reaching out from inside the minibar. It would come and then disappear again quickly; and in those days, deep down, I awaited its arrival eagerly, and even relished the thought of it circling hungrily around me, because I knew I had the battle won before it was started.

The distant tinkling of glasses in the bar—drowsier now, my neighboring columnist having perhaps gone home—and the underwater silence of the room of abandoned readings made me think about shipwrecks again, as though I were already under water, sitting on one of those armchairs bolted to the deck on the *Titanic*. It was better to jump ship while I could still break the spell, and the bell jar in the wax-flower-filled room; before the greenish armchair swallowed me up in its depths, or my notebook, irrevocably blurred, began to float away. I felt nostalgic for the little bedside lamps in my room. The same nostalgia that a man overboard must feel as he sinks, yearning for the ballroom chandeliers and the deck of an ocean liner, all embers and violin chords now and retreating into the pitch-black night.

And sure enough, here are the little lamps, all lit up, and the rain is tapping on the sidewalk. The room next door is still dark; they must have either turned the television off or drawn the curtains. Someone has replaced the almonds in the minibar, taken the bedspread off, and turned down the top sheet on one side of the bed. Double room, single occupancy—a good title for memoirs that nobody will ever ask me to write.

Everything is in order—only they've put two mournful little chocolates on the pillows, in the exact spots where two guests would rest their hypothetical heads. It's a classic trap, and I know exactly what to do in this situation: grab one of them, tear open the wrapper, kick off my shoes, lay down, and pop it in my mouth. I'll rest my head, in fact, on the exact spot where the chocolate was.

A domestic flight less than one hour long, a regional airport that beckoned to you, as they all do, to stay there and let the lives of others flow sweetly past as you keep watch over your newsstand. Before that, a pit stop at the house to change suitcases and somehow finish off the review of the Imperial. And now: another room, another hotel. A whole lifetime, you could say, condensed into just three days (and their three long nights).

Flying affects the memory, too; it's not just a lot of ground that airplanes put between things. I'm surprised by the clarity with which I remember everything that happened in the Imperial that night, because it seems like three years or three centuries have passed. It's as though two identical suitcases got switched on the conveyor belt and I came away with the memories of things that happened to someone else. I feel like I ought to worry about being privy to so many compromising details, and as I comb back through them, I feel the embarrassment, bordering on disgust, of one who finds himself accidentally riffling through the lotions and nail clippers of another person's toiletry bag.

I can already see that this one notebook isn't going to be enough. The computer is useful for articles, but it's been such a long time since I've written anything else that I had forgotten the drawbacks of the blank screen: it makes my mind go blank, too, and discolors my memories. I went out to buy another notepad this morning, in a furtive expedition to the nearest stationery shop.

I'm not familiar with this city, so I followed the directions they gave me at reception. And I haven't set foot outside since then. It's odd, though, in a way: what was it about it that made it seem so furtive to me and made me write that just now, if it was done in broad daylight and with intentions that couldn't possibly be considered by anyone to be anything other than honorable? And who was this "anyone", if not a less sympathetic version of myself, whose disapproving gaze I had felt burning into my back these past three days?

It's an ugly, schoolkid's notebook with a motorcycle rider on the cover. It was the first one they offered me, the cheapest. I didn't want some sophisticated journal, one of those ones that suggest that what is being written in them (and, by extension, the person doing the writing) is important. They didn't have any in that everyday stationery shop, anyhow. I'm under no illusions—I bought the most insignificant notebook in the world in order to hide the significance of having bought it.

I don't know if I slept a long time or hardly at all that afternoon at the Imperial—I had sunk into a black sleep as soon as my head hit the pillow, the moment its bogus, bleach-smelling solace washed over me. I opened my eyes and was blinded by the lamplight. I shut them again, and a negative of the room danced around me in the darkness. My tongue came unstuck from my palate only reluctantly, and as it did so, I became aware of the taste of the little square of chocolate that had still not completely dissolved. Reality took some time to recompose itself: the rain outside; the bathroom; and the whole city around the hotel, too; the hotel; the room next door; the people in the room next door. I can remember that I was having an unpleasant, violent dream: someone was shouting threats into my ear and hitting me.

But someone really was hitting something, someone was shouting. Almost in my ear, in fact, but really it was in the room next door. I sat up, wide awake. On the other side of the partition, a girl—perhaps the one I had seen in her underwear earlier—was shouting. I could hear the voices of the boy and the man who had shut the door, too. I sat there at the edge of the bed. Silence fell. Suddenly the girl cried out—in terror? in rage?—and there was a sound like a whole tower of furniture collapsing against the wall. The head of my bed shook. And that marked a shift: what was happening in the next room over was starting to have effects in mine, and I decided that the aftershock in my bed and the blinking wall lamps gave me license to investigate. I leapt up and quickly found myself in the hallway. It was as deserted as before, and once again in silence. I feared that it would all end there, that the silent hallway and the closed doors would push me back into my room, alone yet again.

But the door next to mine opened and the girl walked out. Not in her underwear—she was wearing a short skirt, and as she walked toward me down the hallway, she was pulling on a T-shirt that obscured her face. She tripped on a crease in the carpet, struggled with the tight T-shirt, and finally managed to get it down over her head. It was indeed the girl I had seen earlier. Now that she was standing and I could see her from close up, she was surprisingly slight, even petite. She looked at me, looked away, then fixed me with her gaze again and didn't let it drop. She seemed angry. She came toward me as though she knew me well and had something to throw in my face. I opened my mouth to say something, even arched my eyebrows. To be honest, it strikes me now that I must have looked like an idiot. But she said nothing at all; she walked past me without stopping, making a beeline for the elevator. I turned around. She didn't even look at me.

"Fuck you."

Fuck *you*, or fuck *him*? Or fuck *them*? I didn't hear her properly, and a moment later she had stepped into the elevator, which was still stopped at our floor where I had left it. Perhaps I hadn't slept much after all, or perhaps there really was no one else staying in the whole hotel. The indifferent doors took five endless seconds to close. This didn't suit her at all. I could just hear her before they closed in front of her.

"Oh for fuck's sake, come on."

She had left the door to 206 half open. No sound came from the other side, only a light that was identical (just like the doorway, just like the crack in it) to that seeping out of my own room. I stood looking at the two doors; they seemed to invite each other's company. I knew that a moment later I would start to have second thoughts, so I strode forward and opened the one that led to my neighbors' room.

Across their little entryway, in their bathroom, all the lights were on. The boy was sitting on the edge of the bathtub with a towel around his waist. A man was holding his chin in one hand and blowing into one of his eyes.

"I don't see anything."

The man whose voice I had heard, clearly. He was older, or at least older-looking, than his voice had made me think.

"But you've got to be more careful. Anything can end up in your eye. It's like an open wound."

I wasn't expecting this quasi-pastoral, even playground-like scene. It didn't match the horrors I had assumed were unfolding in there; I realized then that I had spent the whole afternoon convincing myself something unspeakable was happening in that room. There's a reason I'm not a writer. I realized by the time I was twenty, when I gave up for good on the novel that was so typical of my age, and left it in a drawer: I have a headstrong, trivial imagination. It can't be relied on for serious work. It will dream up convoluted routes for arriving at hum-drum situations, then dive head-first into cliché when something unusual happens (if it really does happen).

In this case, I had my second-rate stock shots at the ready: red streaks all over the mirrors, black puddles on white marble. But the girl in the hallway had no visible wounds, and there was no blood on the bathroom tiles. I couldn't see anything wrong with the boy from where I was standing, either. I stood quietly in the doorway. Neither the boy nor the man turned around. Now, looking back, I'm not sure if they didn't realize I was looking at them or just chose to pretend they didn't. I could hear my heart pounding.

A woman's voice stopped it cold. She sounded perfectly calm.

"What do you want?"

Its owner was coming out of the bedroom. Tall, my age or a little younger. She had on a purple sweater that somehow both invited and repelled the touch of a hand to confirm its color. She spoke without looking at me, balancing on one leg as she fastened the tiny strap of a green leather sandal. She did this—held one leg up and bent back, her long, expert fingers working the clasp on her expensive, almost invisible sandal—with a composure that it was impossible not to admire. These past three days, it's been the first image that comes to mind whenever I think of her.

At last, she looked me in the eye. She had taken her time about it, and I looked away immediately. I preferred not to answer her. Thinking ahead, I first took a look around the room. They were going to throw me out any moment, and I didn't want to be stuck forever with the unsolved mystery of that room that was about to vanish just like that into thin air—furniture, people, and all— like something out of a fairy tale.

The room had, of course, all the things I had already seen through the crack in the door, the things that were also in my matching room. And things that weren't the same, like in a game of spot the difference: the armchairs and the little table were there, but upturned and hurled against the wall; the bed was there, but no gray bedspread. And almost no sheets or blankets, either, as they were in a heap at the foot of the bed. On the other hand, it did look as though the joyless signed etchings on the walls were identical to the ones in my room. The lamps at the head of the bed, like the ones in my room, were switched on.

But they looked dim, because from about the height of the woman's shoulder shone the bright spotlight of a digital camera mounted on a tripod. It was difficult to tell if the light made the room and the bed bigger or more compact—they were thrown out of shape, just as the presence of the camera distorted the possible significances of the situation. It made the stains on the mattress, which clearly predated the remodeling, stand out very plainly. In that light, they loomed large in their yawning nudity. Or rather, their prudery—hotel mattresses are one of those things that are not made to be seen, and never should be.

The woman's question wasn't a question. In fact, it nipped any possible conversation in the bud. In the bathroom, the man was still leaning over the boy, who hadn't gotten up. The two of them looked at me without saying a word and didn't seem any more surprised than she.

And even though I would have preferred to take it as a real question in order to buy some time, it was difficult to hit on a decent response. What *did* I want, in fact? It was hard to say. What did I expect, as I stood there in that room, from these three people staring at me in silence? For lack of anything better to say, I ended up giving the details that she (almost as much as I) would surely have preferred I keep to myself: I was in the room next door, I'd heard shouting and banging noises, gone out into the hallway, found the door open, wondered if anyone was hurt.

She gave me a serious look. A furious or perhaps amused spark flashed in her eyes and then vanished. Or not so much in her eyes as around them—we talk about eyes, but what we read really goes on in what's around them: in the eyebrows, the eyelids, in the untold bundles of nameless muscles that tighten the corners to close them, or that sit in the fraction of cheek beneath them.

I like to think she at least understood that I, too, thought it unnecessary to polish up those run-of-the-mill lies into anything else. In the bathroom, the man snorted. It looked as though he was going to say something, but she beat him to it.

"Well, thank you. But everything's fine. Good night."

The woman smiled politely, and there was a mocking look in her eyes now for sure. Was she laughing at me for being a coward? She was happily playing my game, while still looking down on me for resorting to it.

I hesitated. I looked into the bathroom again, avoiding eye contact with the boy and the man; then around the bedroom, at the tripod and the camera pointed at the bed. She took another step forward.

"Good night."

The man in the bathroom straightened up.

That was all there was to say.

"Good night."

Or all I felt able to say, at least. I turned around to walk out of the room; before I could close the door, that deserted hallway, the little pictures in their cheap luxury frames, and the carpet all weighed down on me at once.

"Wait."

I turned around, feeling saved. I looked at her, trying not to give the slightest gesture that might make things easier for her. I could already tell she was the proud sort.

"Have you informed reception? Is somebody on their way up?"

That hurt—the question, and the fact she was so formal with me. Did she really think me capable of such a thing?

"No."

I held her gaze until it was her turn, for the first time, to lower her eyes.

"Of course I haven't called them."

I said it faintly, and even I thought my "Of course" sounded incongruous. Why "Of course"? What was so obvious about it if we didn't know each other at all?

No one said anything more. I waited a while, until there was nothing for it but to go back out into the deserted hallway. Looking back, I like to think that she knew very well I hadn't informed anyone, that I'm not the type to go running to reception. And I like to think that we shared the "Of course"—what she had really said when she asked me whether I had told reception was, "Of course you haven't."

But I didn't think any of this at the time. Just as I was closing the door, the last tiny particle of chocolate came loose from my gums. The taste started in one corner of my palate, spread quickly through my mouth, effervesced, and then died out in less than a second, without leaving a trace; it was already the trace of a trace. But it was enough to remind me of the other little chocolate— the one that still lay untouched on my pillow— and of the virginal half of my bed, the bedsheets still unwrinkled. The ghost of the chocolate in my mouth, a vision of the room without me; I turned around, opened the door again, and walked into the entryway.

She hadn't moved. She didn't react.

"I was here earlier. This afternoon."

She didn't so much as raise her impenetrable eyebrows.

"Oh yes?"

In the bathroom, the boy leapt to his feet, holding his towel on with one hand.

"Close the door."

I turned around to do as she had said. I was still holding the handle.

"Not you, him."

She walked over to the bathroom herself and shut the door on some surprised looks from the boy and the man.

"Just a sec. I'll let you guys know when I'm done."

Then she turned to face me. She seemed like another person altogether, suddenly, when she smiled.

"I'm not going to be so easygoing with you quite yet."

She turned her back on me and walked into the bedroom. I followed her, weighing up that "yet."

"We can talk here. Even though it's rather a mess."

The air in the room was thick. There were empty miniature bottles of gin and whiskey on the bedside table and the bed. The porn actors continued their exertions silently on the television screen. She gestured to the only armchair that was still in its place.

"Have a seat. I'll open the window."

I sat down while she turned off the TV and the spotlight on the camera. The room itself also felt a little less hostile in the lamplight. Cool air and the sound of rain came in from the street. She sat back down on the edge of the unmade bed.

"And how is that?"

How was what? It took me a moment to understand that she was taking up the conversation from the last words we had spoken in the hallway.

"They made a mistake at reception. They gave me the key to this room."

She looked at me impassively.

"And what did you see?"

"Hardly anything. I wasn't here long. The boy." I jutted my chin toward the bathroom. "And the girl who walked out."

"Right."

She hesitated before adding anything further.

"They fought. She got very upset."

She said it quickly, apparently without much interest in hiding the fact that it was a spurious explanation, that it didn't explain a thing, really, or do anything other than state the obvious.

I would have liked to ask her why, but I didn't feel I had the right to—nor would she have been obliged to answer. Or would she? She had the opposite effect on me to my neighboring columnist: with her, I wasn't sure if we had established the necessary trust. She spoke first.

"Are you with the police?"

I smiled. If I had been offended that she had taken me for a snitch before, I ought to be even more put out now. But the question amused me.

"No."

"And you're not the hotel security guard?"

I looked down and was pleased to find a rock-solid alibi.

"I'm not even wearing shoes."

We looked at each other and laughed a little.

"Well, be careful. A glass got broken and there are pieces of it on the floor. I had to put shoes on myself."

She spoke with tentative good-will. I ventured a little more.

"I'm here to review the hotel."

I regretted it the moment the words were out of my mouth. It sounded forced, and I thought it unlikely she would tolerate that sort of pseudo-friendliness. And perhaps it would be worse if she did. I never talk about my work with strangers. It only leads to stupid conversations. I feared I would now be the one who had to put together some tedious explanation.

"To review it?"

She didn't give me time to resign myself to answering, hardly even to nod.

"What's your byline?"

I wasn't expecting that. Perhaps that's what it would always be like, talking to her. She reminded you that almost everything people say to each other is nothing but a mechanical testing of the waters. When she heard my name, she leaned back, grinning.

"Oh, of course it is. I read your column. I've even followed a few of your recommendations."

I remember very well that it was then that she started to speak to me like an equal. And that I felt a prick of foolish pride even a little more intense than usual.

"Oh really?"

And at the same time, I started to feel impatient. A conversation like that was absurd given the context. I know myself well, and I've learned to resign myself to the fact that well-aimed questions and witty parries only occur to me after the horse has bolted. But even now, I can't think of a topic of conversation that wouldn't have been ridiculous at that moment. I didn't know what I had gone in there to talk to her about. I had no reason to stay in that room. I didn't want to stay, and I didn't want to leave. I'm not surprised now that I started to feel faintly irritated—not with her, but with myself.

I looked at the furniture again, at the camera, at the little empty bottles. I couldn't see a speck of broken glass. She got up and closed the window slowly. She no longer seemed in a hurry.

"And what are you going to say about this one?"

"I'll say they ought to have better soundproofing."

The joke came out of the blue. It told itself, really. I can't even claim I said it to see her reaction. Although it was interesting to watch it, anyway. She turned around quickly. For a brief second, her eyes smiled as they had earlier. It flattered her to smile like that, in a negative image of my page neighbor: her mouth serious, and all her intention in her eyes. She made no comment.

"Well, you've already seen what I do."

I pretended to go along with the joke. It was easier to say it jokingly.

"Porn?"

She laughed, and I assumed—wrongly—that that would be her whole reply.

"That's right. Well, almost."

She spoke seriously, almost pensively. Without defiance. I could see that it was now she who feared the string of irksome questions—she looked at her hands, adjusted a switch on the camera that didn't need adjusting. The bathroom door creaked open. We both turned around as the boy walked in wearing his towel. She seemed thankful for the interruption. I was glad that something had happened, too, that the boy had come in. But before it was too late, I gave her a protesting look. I wanted to make it clear that I wasn't going to ask her stupid questions, either. Now I think my look may have had a pleading edge to it.

We stayed like that for a long second and a half. (Were we understanding each other? Or am I imagining all that now?) And then she looked over at the boy, who was standing by the door.

"Sorry. I'm just gonna get dressed and I'll go."

The boy brushed past without looking at me on his way over to the bed. He fished a pair of pants out of the tangle of sheets. Then he knelt down and felt along the floor under the mattress. He brought out some underpants, shook them, and after a lot of fussy maneuvering managed to put them on before taking off his towel. Up close and in profile he was less bulky than I'd thought.

She held out his shirt to him with one hand.

"I'll finish up with you in a moment."

The other man appeared in the doorway and took me completely off guard. I'd forgotten that he was also in the room. It quickly became clear that I was the odd one out here. It was as though common sense had walked in, leaned against the doorframe, and given me a knowing look. I almost jumped up out of my armchair. The woman was looking for something in the drawers of the bedside table.

"Well, I'll be going."

She turned around, and it almost seemed she had forgotten about me. She smiled with only her mouth.

"To tell you the truth, I can't even offer you a drink."

She nodded toward the empty minibar. I would have enjoyed getting to turn down an invitation to stay.

She was looking at the man. When I turned around, I caught him making an impatient gesture.

"OK, well, good night."

The boy didn't even look up from his position on the edge of the bed; he was utterly absorbed in the task of tying the laces on his sneakers. I think there was something unnatural about how natural he was: he combined rudeness, awkwardness, and an anxious, shy desire to cover his tracks.

I brushed past the other man on my way to the door. He didn't move or bother to hide his disparaging look. When I was in the entryway, I heard her voice again.

"But if you haven't drunk all of yours yet, you can invite me over to your room."

I stood very still, focused on concealing the fact that I'd been caught off guard again.

"I say your room because the hotel bar's a bit depressing … funereal, as you might say."

And I had said it. Or thought it, at least. And written it down in this very notebook, I now see on rereading. She must have seen in my face that my guard was down, because she smiled a little. It was a serious joke, apparently.

"Then I can tell you more about all this."

For the second time, this woman was saving me from my desolate room, from the hypocritical top sheet turned down on one side of the bed. She didn't wait for me to reply.

"Great. I'll be right over."

She smiled and continued rummaging in the drawers. The boy was just about finished putting his clothes on: a baggy T-shirt covered his chest, stomach, and belly button in turn. It bore the serious, utterly incongruous logo of an insurance company. The other man still said nothing. I threw him the most insolent "See you later" I could muster and closed the door behind me.

The Hotel Life

Tunnel in time or bottomless pit? Riding on the prestige of illustrious guests past can be risky. This week we travel south with our critic for an emergency visit to the Reina Amalia Hotel.

THE SCOTTISH POET'S ROOM

Time and hotels are pitted against each other in a game we don't understand. The rules must be complicated. We don't live long enough to earn the right to play, or to develop the perspective necessary to take the upper hand. We know they've always been betting against each other, but only they know what the stakes and conditions are.

Sometimes it seems more like a race: a hundred years ago, a brand-new hotel would plant a piece of the future in a place where nothing had happened for centuries. Least of all time— time who discovered, to its annoyance, that it had to rush out to the small, provincial town or the clearing in the jungle that it had taken its eye off, thinking it already had things perfectly wrapped up there.

Occasionally, time will get even by giving a poisoned gift to hotels: it will set them to one side and then quicken its own pace until they become islands without ports, swamps where the years that have kept flowing cruelly by outside stagnate and start to smell just a little bit too sweet.

At first, this will appear to be a blessing: even the dullest door handle comes into the world with a secret deadline for redeeming itself. And an expiration date too, unfortunately: one fine day, the sad trap will spring that causes latches to jam, drains to clog, light switches to stick, and the air of lounges where forgotten liturgies were once held to become unbreathable.

The Reina Amalia Hotel has already half lost its own bet. It's some time now since the main facade gave up the fight, and now it looks straight out at the miserable town that grew up awkwardly around it, ceasing to attract the picturesque, turn-of-the-century pilgrims. But the back of the building continues to impose its confused, Bavarian profile (which was either modern or absurd in its day, according to the taste of the visitor; then dated; and now inevitable) on the landscape.

The river that cut its groove millions of years ago and that runs dry for six months of the year; the barren, African plains; the unbroken sea that one spies doubtfully in the distance: thanks to highly precise happenstance, every housing development along the coastline is hidden by a hill that obscures it from the view of the hotel's back-yard stroller.

It's an unreasoning landscape, as though everything that had ever come to pass there since the Roman Empire—and everything that has literally passed it by—were a strange dream in a lingering siesta. After textbook battles, after incomprehensible schisms and councils, and whole centuries

74

with nothing to write up, only the hotel has managed to make a mark on it.

The rooms at the front command a view of apartment blocks and the oasis of antennae that dominate the deserted parking lot. Clearly, our present is the future of the old, bewildered hotel.

I write to you from one of the rooms at the rear, and it wasn't easy or cheap to get. But the sentimental traveler should be sure to ask for one—never was such frankly abusive overpricing so justified. From here you can see the overgrown garden and the same stark landscape that was surveyed by the Portuguese queen who inaugurated the hotel and gave it her name. She brought with her a whole train of Regenerationists, who saw the place as a symbol for a thousand and one things. Personally, I had never before seen anything so stubbornly resistant to symbolism as this charmless plain.

And, of course, there's the Scottish poet who spent two months shut up in his room here, shocking half the continent with his grief-stricken letters. It's a clear case of an author ahead of his time—how email would have helped him in his efforts to appoint himself poet laureate of his distant, doleful country.

At reception they tell me they've kept the original furniture in his room. There is apparently a different occupant, however; it's not easy to visit, and as I write this week's review (newspapers, as you know, do not wait), I don't know whether I'll be able to see it to tell the tale. I'm on the same floor, three balconies over. We can at least assume that I can see from my window more or less the same thing that can be seen from the window that was his.

And, of course, the very same landscape that the man himself must have seen. But not for long. And that is not because I am only going to stay for one night; nor is it because new housing

75

developments are going to colonize every last embankment on this side, there being more than enough dull, featureless plain on the other.

Rather, it is because the hotel will cease to be a hotel; it will even cease to look out over this landscape. Here and there, I have heard tell of the possible closure and not unlikely demolition of the Reina Amalia. And so here you have me, filing this review ahead of the ultimate deadline. And wondering if this installment of "The Hotel Life" ought not to be called "The Hotel Death".

Forgive the joke—for being morbid and, what's worse, for being weak and far-fetched. But what can I say: almost all of them end up being like that, almost always.

I managed to salvage the review of the Imperial at the last minute, but only out of a sense of professionalism. And this one isn't going to come out well, either. I can see it, and they'll see it at the paper too, of course, although they probably won't say anything. They never criticize or congratulate—one thing makes up for the other after all these years. It's a bleak but efficient method. And the past guarantees my future; I've got some margin, some wiggle-room, I'd say, for a few bad articles.

Perhaps too wide a margin, too much wiggle-room. I thought I had chosen a trade with no expiration date, but I may have been wrong: this hotel's fate may yet be mine own, too.

Now that I write this, it feels as though the five minutes I spent in her room were longer than the hour or so she spent in mine. I confess that I waited for her that night without ever quite thinking she would come, and I was surprised when she did. Oddly, it may have been even more surprising than it would be to hear her knocking at this door now that there are not just a few yards between us but probably hundreds or thousands of miles. I would pretend to be surprised, though, I'd fake a little start—for my sake as well as hers, out of simple respect for good form. But beneath that, I would feel it was the natural thing for her to do. And perhaps it was. Why pretend that we are privy to the laws that dictate what can and cannot happen, if deep down we all know that, ultimately, we collude in the consummation of everything, of the things we desire the most and the things we fear the most? We don't even need to desire a thing much—sometimes it's enough to simply think about it, in occasional snatches of free time, for a few days.

Of course, everything in my room was as it had been five minutes before: the lamps, the antagonizing chocolate, my shoes at the foot of the bed like little mausoleum dogs. It couldn't have been any other way, but it somehow surprised me that these things had remained their identical selves, determined to prove that, indeed, only five minutes had passed. And that during that time they had neither done nor felt a thing.

I put my shoes on, checked there was enough of everything left in the minibar, and poured myself a whiskey. The alcohol warmed my insides and brought me back into the feel of the room. My hands still felt cold, but after the second sip, they stopped shaking.

I walked around the room, trying to look at it with the eyes of the woman who would soon be looking at it herself. The mattress in her room, obscenely on display; the rumpled sheets on the half of the bed where I'd slept; the other half smooth, with its turned-down top sheet and pillow, both immaculate: three stages of the hotel life that would inevitably have to be retraced. Or anticipated—perhaps my bed would end up like the one next door. I couldn't tell if my visitor was on her way over here in order to end up lying in it. In truth, the woman hadn't done anything that would give rise to the question. Apart from directing porn movies, that is (*Well, almost*, she had said). That was no reason to assume anything, of course. But there are some questions that ask themselves, that cut to the head of the line instead of waiting as they would if they had any sense. At that moment, for example, I still hadn't asked myself if I wanted to sleep with her. Now, that seems odd to me.

I suppose she must have knocked on the door just as I was about to consider the matter. Only to find the answer and realize my mind was quite made up—the questions I want to sit down and ask myself almost always turn out to be answered already.

Hers were not the two taps, gentle but heavy with meaning, of the lover who knows she will be welcomed. Nor the playful Morse code that invites or presupposes the trivial reply from the other side. Still less the four knocks of Fate itself at the door that open the Fifth Symphony—that would have seemed too noirish, or worse, theatrical. And from the little time we had spent talking, it was clear she was not one for melodrama.

They were three short, neutral knocks that would have been the envy of the most professional room service.

"Hi."

She walked confidently into the room, with a smile that was different from all her previous ones. It was professional, too: a business smile, a smile for paying calls. A doctor's house call, almost. If I think about the woman now, I realize that the first thing I see floating through the air is that self-contained, precisely calibrated curve.

With that smile, she guessed, formulated, and answered—right from the beginning and better than I ever could have—the question I hadn't yet managed to ask myself: we were not going to sleep together in that bed. And that might also have contained the answer to my second question, the one I only asked myself later and continue to ask myself now; perhaps that way she had of putting the question to rest is what stopped me from clearly desiring the opposite. We talked a lot that night about people sleeping together, and now I'm amazed to remember how effortlessly she avoided the inevitable fact: that the possibility of our doing the same might flutter through the room at any point.

Of all the things there were to see in my room (not much, of course, compared to hers), she only had eyes for my whiskey.

"I'll have one, too, see if I can catch up with you."

"Sure."

She carried on talking while I took ice, glass, and a bottle out of the minibar.

"Thanks for inviting me over. Or for letting me invite myself. As you saw, my room's a mess; this way I can give Pedro some time to tidy it up."

I passed her the glass. She took it without touching me, raised it a little, smiled, and didn't drink from it.

"Which one's Pedro?"

"The older one. To tell you the truth, I can't remember the other one's name. The boy. We just met him today."

We were still standing, facing each other, glasses in hand. I think we both understood at the same time how the whole thing risked becoming absurd in that arrangement.

"We can sit down, if you like."

She was already taking her seat.

"So. I also wanted to thank you for trying to help. There was no need—but all the same. And for not calling reception. That's why I came."

I thought I caught some emphasis on the *That's why*. It irritated me.

"No need to thank me. And I don't think that's why you came."

It sounded as bad to me then as it does now looking back—straight from the opening scene of the kind of porn they were shooting, or had at least paid to watch on TV, next door. And yet I hadn't meant to insinuate anything. I wanted to remind her that a few minutes ago she had promised to tell me more. She gave me an amused look.

"Well. That *is* why I came. But not the only reason. Bearing in mind what you saw earlier when you snuck in this afternoon …"

"I didn't sneak in. They got mixed up downstairs."

"But I think you drew out the mix-up. And you must want to know what this is all about. And why I read your reviews. Which I like very much, by the way, I'm not sure if I mentioned that before. Did I mention it? You've got to admit that there's something funny about the whole situation. It deserves a nightcap together, don't you think?"

Did it deserve one? Perhaps it did, according to some universally accepted scale that everyone but me knows by heart and uses as matter of course. She handed me a business card.

"This is my company. It's a website, as you can see."

There was nothing but a web address: www.thehotellife.com. I read the unexpected name out loud to buy myself some time. She laughed.

"That's right—I lead a hotel life, too."

I looked at her, not knowing what to say.

"I hope you don't mind. I'd like to say I named it as an homage, but that wouldn't be entirely true. I chose it when I was setting up the page, five years ago, kind of off the cuff. The guy who was designing it needed a name for the test page; what I do is related to hotels, too, and I remembered your column. We checked, and you didn't have the domain name registered. You missed a chance there, by the way, that could have really worked out for you. And in the end, I just kept it. I asked, and they said there was no issue with the rights, that the phrase was in the public domain. And it can't be changed now."

I couldn't tell if the use of the name was flattering or a veiled slight. I opted for asking why it couldn't be changed now.

"Well, I can tell from the face you're making that you're not familiar with it, but since it launched, the page has been really successful. A week doesn't go by without someone writing to me saying that thehotellife. com has been voted 'Best Erotic Page Of The Year' or 'recognized for its contribution to online racial diversity.' Apparently, they even study it at universities. A few years ago, this really quiet girl who had posed for us sent me a whole 'process documentation' thing—turned out it was a project for a Galician contemporary arts center. They invited me to the opening. I didn't go, but I was pleased. So I need to keep the name as it is—considering how difficult it is to establish a strong brand, I'd be crazy to change it. I owe it to my audience."

She looked at me seriously after that remark. The off-the-wall adjectives my neighboring columnist uses in his reviews came to mind. Even now, it's difficult to tell if her serious tone was a joke. I'd prefer to think it was, even if she could very well be the sort of person who is capable of saying something like that without a glimmer of irony. We have to make ourselves distrust the impression that we can know a stranger perfectly. I like someone who can tell a good joke, but that's the easy bit. You don't know somebody until you've seen what he takes seriously. Many with an impeccable resume for irony will end up putting a foot wrong and lapsing into awful, plodding earnestness sooner or later. I spoke into my whiskey glass.

"And what's on the site?"

"Guys like the kid you saw today. Well, guys and girls. You know, the typical repertoire: people on their own, people in couples or in groups. They're always amateurs, though. And always in hotel rooms, a different one every time. It's a really saturated market, you've got to stand out. And people get a kick out of the hotel thing— they like to see the world a bit, compare bedrooms and bathrooms. That's our trademark. To get all the photos and videos you have to subscribe and pay a monthly fee. It's not much though, you'd be surprised. All above board. We always ask the models for at least two forms of ID to be sure they're eighteen or older. We keep copies in the office just in case 'the authorities' come and ask for them one day. Although to tell you the truth, they've given no signs of life up to now. When we started, I thought there would be someone watching everything we did online, but these days I don't even think about it most of the time. Maybe some day the police will call me, or I'll get a summons in the mail, or in an email. Maybe one of our models' significant others will turn up one day to 'have a little chat.' For a moment, earlier, that's who I thought you might be, actually."

She scarcely smiled at her own joke. You could tell she was in a hurry to carry on telling me her story. If indeed it was me she was telling it to. She was speaking into her glass, too. Perhaps she'd forgotten I was in the room.

"So that's about the size of it for now. And in the meantime, the page has really taken off. Especially with people who only speak Spanish. There's a lot of competition from the Americans, but we carved out a niche in the market for ourselves pretty quickly. And it wasn't just luck. I knew there was no reason porn should be any different from movies or soap operas—sometimes, even if it's just for a nice change, people like to see how the things the Americans do are being done in their own language, too. So if you're the first one to start something new and you run the business well, you're unlikely to get knocked off your perch. Like everything else, people have their habits when it comes to porn, and they want convenience—they can't spend all day at it. We professionals are here to make things easier for them."

My page neighbor had said something similar. Perhaps he would have accepted this woman as belonging to our own trade in some broad sense. Anyway, judging by what she told me and what I've seen since, she's a real professional in her field. She told me that she now has a staff of ten working on the site, as well as the actors, the casting team, and the film crew. They're often all on the road, looking for actors and something new to offer people: new faces, new hotel rooms. She also told me that in porn, everything needs to be changing a little bit—but not too much—all the time.

"At the beginning, I did it all myself, and when I was looking for actors, I got more than one nasty response, and even several insults. Then I realized it was all a question of practice. Pretty soon, it becomes easy to see who's going to like the idea and say yes. A lot of the people I've talked to lately have already heard about the site or have even looked at it. I'm not sure why I say 'even,' though, because it's not like there's much difference between hearing about a website and looking at it. With the internet, no one needs to stay curious about anything for long. A lot of people write and send in photos spontaneously, although fewer than one in fifty actually make the cut. Individuals put themselves forward as models—but also couples and even groups and families. They invite us to visit their city, or offer to pay for their own trip out. Some of them very kindly recommend hotels to us. But I prefer to do the casting in advance and send somebody to prepare everything. To do the scouting, as they say in the movie business."

She looked up at me again and smiled. Then she changed her tone, like someone hurrying to the end of an awkward or boring speech. I wasn't bored, and I don't think I looked it, but I understood why she was in a hurry. I know these hotel conversations all too well. Lone travelers fall into them easily—in the bar, or the elevator, or the armchairs in the lobby during those fearful forty-five minutes before dinnertime. I tend to sidestep them, myself, but I've eavesdropped on a lot of them. Confidences are abruptly cut off, or else continued in someone's room. In our case, the former might come to pass at any moment. But the second option was impossible—we were already in the place where chats like that wind up. And the truth is, as I am forever making my way through hotels (and, more so than anyone else, just passing through), I've never worked out what those encounters are supposed to lead to the next day, after the sojourn upstairs: At that moment, I could have used a map just to find my way around my own room. Perhaps she was less lost than me.

"So that's how it goes. I could run the business from home. But working in an office is boring, and I've got people who are better at it. We're selling more and more ad space all the time. We even have T-shirts. They're pretty popular, apparently. People are selling them on eBay."

She paused, and I thought perhaps I was supposed to reply. The whiskey was making her more talkative. It made me reluctant to speak. And actually, now I'm glad I didn't say much that evening. She didn't seem to mind.

"I never found traveling for pleasure very pleasurable. When I travel for no reason, I end up going a bit crazy. You tie yourself up in knots over decisions that are tiny but can suddenly turn tragic—whether to have a siesta or not, whether to go to the museum or to the park. Does that happen to you? Now I've always got something to do—a place to go to, and a reason to go there. Pedro comes with me to help me out with the other camera. And to help me generally. Sometimes stuff can get a bit out of hand, and he's great at getting things under control. What do you think?"

I sat up in the armchair. It was precisely the question that would be most difficult to answer. I decided to buy a bit of time.

"What do I think of Pedro?"

"No, I mean what do you think of the whole thing. I imagine you don't think much of Pedro. He's not the friendliest guy, and actually, it's his job not to be. He gets rid of snitches, peeping Toms and weirdos for us."

"Ah."

She laughed and got up.

"I didn't mean you were a weirdo. A peeping Tom, maybe."

She was looking for two more bottles of whiskey in the minibar. She spoke without looking at me, her head still halfway inside the fridge.

"Did you like what you saw?"

I stared into my glass. I let her empty another miniature bottle into it. I took a drink and let her question spread out and slip down my throat with it. So, really, it was going to be me who had to try and catch up with her. I made a sincere effort to reply. I've thought about the answer since, but I still haven't come up with a convincing one. Now, I realize she was asking the wrong question.

Or simply an unfair one. I talk, you listen; I choose the topics, you introduce some variations—that was the pattern that had been established in our conversation up to that point. Once someone has set the tone in conversations like this one (which always happens very quickly, during the first few exchanges, or even before a single word has been spoken), it's difficult to force a change. For me, it was actually the ideal solution: I could think through all of this later. I would know what I thought—whether or not I liked what I saw and heard—later, when I wrote it all down. I was deceiving myself, of course. In fact, I think it was a way of deceiving her, too—I'm writing now about what happened and I still don't understand it. And I could already tell, then, that that was how it would be.

"I told you, I hardly saw anything: the kid wasn't getting turned on, he was cold … and then that man Pedro shut the door, and I left. I didn't even realize you were in the room."

She looked me in the eye. I think she was trying to calculate the extent to which it might be I, and not she, who was really calling the shots in the conversation. Because that's what this conversation was partly about, or mostly about—like all conversations.

I watched her weigh up how worthwhile it would be to break our unspoken agreement and go to the trouble of getting me to answer her question without any stalling, as directly as she had asked it. Or at least I imagine that's what she was doing; perhaps all she wanted from me that night were enough answers for her to shape her monologue around and give it the appearance of a conversation.

Now I think (and perhaps I thought it at the time, too, and then forgot) that, just as I do in mine, she must have to speak to a lot of people in her line of work without having a real conversation with any of them. Perhaps she's forgotten how it's done. Or was never very interested in doing it, or lost what interest she had as she met more and more people and discovered that their apparently endless variety in fact boils down to a handful of possible combinations of the same tired old gambits.

In any case, after a short silence, she let slide the fact that I was avoiding the question and carried on talking. I can't tell if she was being a little more or a little less astute than me at that point.

"Right. Today was a disaster. They were useless. We'll have to see if we can cut anything good from it."

"What happened after that? Why did the girl get angry?"

"Well, you must have seen she's got a temper on her. She was nervous, and the kid wasn't doing a great job. And I'll admit that I don't have a lot of patience anymore. Sometimes I forget that, for the actors, every session is the first session. Well it's too bad for her. She left before getting paid."

"Paid?"

She laughed again.

"Of course. The models get paid. It's one thing for them not to have done this before, but it would be another one entirely if they didn't get paid for it. I'm upfront with them about that before we get started—it makes things easier. And she was the one most interested in the money, too. The kid just wanted to be in a movie."

"Didn't you pay him?"

"Yeah, sure, of course I paid him. But he wasn't really concerned about the money, although he pretended it was really important to him. It's like that with a lot of them, although it ought to be the opposite; they think the fact that there's money involved cleans the whole thing up. That it makes it all a bit more noble—or less sordid, anyway. So."

A silence followed. Perhaps, if I'd answered her question, if I had made an effort to say whether I'd liked what I'd seen (or what I had liked of everything I'd seen), the conversation would have continued down that road and we would have gotten to philosophizing. But I doubt it—that didn't seem to be her style, and now it seems even less so. But she appeared to notice that my precautions forced her to take some of her own. It made me angry to think that I might have disappointed her.

Or rather, it made me angry that it made me angry—my being in the position of the person who will either satisfy or disappoint decisively gave her the upper hand.

But she already had the upper hand, anyway. That's clear to me now that I remember how, when she said "So" again while brusquely getting up from her chair, I suddenly felt a burning desire for her to stay, a desire free from doubt or precaution, a silent groan that surprised even me.

And she did stay. She walked over to the desk and turned to look at me.

"I've got an idea. Do you have a pen? There aren't any here. These new hotels have lost the good old habits."

I held out to her the one I am writing with now. With a smile, she jotted a few numbers in the margin of one of the hotel brochures.

"Here's a password to get into my site. It's like a universal subscription, and it won't ever expire. You can get into any of the sections with this, including the paying ones, of course, which are where the good stuff is. Like the master key they gave you at reception. It's the one I use, and a few other special members, and now you."

She handed me the slip of paper, and I left it on the bedside table without looking at it—it would have been like counting a tip. I didn't thank her, but only because I was caught off guard. That really irritates me now, even though I don't think she thought much of it; she smiled and suddenly seemed resolved to start liking me, or else to keep liking me, come Hell or high water. I didn't like that, either because it was less than I had hoped for or because it slyly reintroduced the question of who had the advantage. Apparently, liking me would be her revenge.

"It'd be an honor if you returned the visit. Even if it is just virtually. It seems only fair—I've got the advantage, after all."

I must have looked taken aback. She hadn't read my mind, but apparently we were thinking in the same terms. She smiled.

"Because I've read *you*, you see. It doesn't make much sense to sit here talking to you about what I do if you haven't seen it. And as you know, it's truer in my business than in any other that a picture is worth a thousand words. That's what it's all about, in the end."

She sat down again.

"Even if I never was interested in offering just the photos on their own. It's odd, but they're not enough. You always need at least one line, a carefully chosen little paragraph. That guy, the web designer? He hadn't read a book since he left school, he listened to me talk and talk and then ignored everything I told him. And yet he's still a subscriber after all these years. He's practically the oldest customer. So I imagine he's worked out by now that what I write does matter, in the end. It's what sets us apart."

Her passion for clichés caught me off guard again. She sat up and laughed.

"So, you know, if you need a bit of extra work."

We both laughed. Then we both took a long sip from our drinks at the same time, then we laughed again. I give her all the credit and admit she had a knack for cunningly working a new note into the conversation. We talked about my work, about the hotel, about hotels in general. Like me, she enjoys the big ones, and any that have a long track record. And failing that, she would always choose an impersonal establishment over a charming boutique hotel. We agreed that it's a scourge, charm. I provide the charm, I remember her saying. She chose the hotels carefully when she was preparing her work trips—she liked to handle that part herself. For her own enjoyment and for practical considerations: she would rather the staff be efficient than friendly, that they have enough experience to have seen a few things, that they be discreet, and not keep track of all the people coming into the room or knock on the door every five minutes. We both lamented the progressive extinction of that particular species of hotel professional.

And she thought that at least some, if not all of her subscribers appreciated her careful choice of the right hotels. She had had emails applauding her taste in selecting a particular room, or a view just visible through a window in the background. So porn, too—porn especially, perhaps—had its connoisseurs.

And it's for them that she really does her work. She doesn't give the names of the establishments, she told me, nor does she shoot anything outside the rooms (although they had, on occasion, ventured briefly out into a hallway to film a preamble at the door into a room). And she's never had a complaint addressed to her from a single hotel—either no one working there has seen the site; or if they have seen it, they don't recognize the hotel; or else they recognize it but prefer not to let on.

She likes to imagine they've decided that it can't be bad publicity for the place, in the end. She'll never know, though, because she never goes back to a city or a hotel.

"If you go to the site, you'll see that when I visit a city where you've reviewed a hotel, I tend to stay in that one. Our work isn't all that different, really."

I smiled. It had just occurred to me that, like me, she must make reservations under a fake name. They were similar in that way, too.

"You think so?"

"Yes. Although I can see from your face that you don't agree. And that's not all. Sometimes after reading your articles, I've wanted to take up a few things with you. I remember a horrible write-up you gave to a hotel in the Azores that I had liked a lot. You spent half a page attacking the 'cosmetic freebies' in the bathroom. I could have killed you."

I laughed. I remembered that review. And she was right: the hotel was excellent. It had a garden that was practically a park, and a steaming, sulphurous hot spring filled with yellow water, inside a bathhouse covered in faded mosaics. But I arrived there off the back of a long, chaotic trip I had made for a special edition paid for by the Portuguese board of tourism. A half-hearted fling across a string of islands, a fling forged from silly coincidences and scant enthusiasm, had finally fallen apart there, leaving a bitter taste in my mouth. Throughout that stay, I had felt at my back the same threat of ferocious sadness that had raised its head in the reading room that night and that I could almost hear pacing around the door to the room now, waiting for her to leave.

I told her she was right, that I'd been very tired when I wrote it. She was prodding a little cube of ice down into her whisky. It was very small by now, almost entirely melted. She would submerge it gently, let it surface, and push it down again.

"We're all tired, aren't we?"

Then she got up, smiling. It was the same smile as I'd seen at the beginning of the evening—as though we had scarcely talked at all, or as if nothing had been said that deserved any other sort of smile.

"And we're right to be. It must be after three o'clock. And I don't know about you, but I have to get up early tomorrow. Or today, rather."

At the time, I assumed her indifference was feigned. Now I'm not so sure. She was right, it was very late. And actually, she was right about everything else. You could see how confident she was in that. She was irritatingly self-assured, which of course only made her more attractive.

We looked at each other without speaking. In fact, it was that second of silence that made me doubtful, and that still makes me doubtful now. A hotel expert like herself couldn't have failed to imagine what I was imagining—and, finally, very definitely desiring—at that moment. I felt an anxiety that I only became aware of when I realized I had pictured being relieved of it: whatever happened, sooner or later she would close the door behind her and I would be left alone and would sit here and write it all down in this notebook.

It was a cowardly sort of relief. Writing is for cowards, in my opinion. I stood up too.

"Well, we'll read each other soon."

She quickly finished her drink as she said this and set the glass down on the bedside table. I couldn't tell if her farewell was genuine. I held her gaze, and couldn't help thinking to myself (in these exact words, absurd as that was): "This isn't going to last." And it didn't last. It stopped lasting when I had the thought, or because I had it. I hesitated another second longer, and it proved to be the fateful second—it may have been the exact one that decided it for her.

"Pedro must have finished tidying up by now. I'd better leave you. It's very late."

I said nothing, paralyzed as though in a bad dream. Eventually she held out her hand, and I managed to offer her mine.

It wasn't a cold handshake, or a warm one, or full of double meanings. It meant nothing more than it was supposed to mean: that we had met, that we had talked, that we were now shaking hands to say goodbye.

"Goodbye."

"Goodbye."

She left the room, closing the door carefully. It now no longer seemed an acceptable revenge to sit and write this down and make more sense of it all.

There's no internet in the rooms at the Reina Amalia—another sign of its being resigned to its own future. Or of its lack of faith in the future, period—this hotel lives on bottling the past. When I asked about it, checking in at reception, they presented the drawback as a gift, even as a response to the demands of their clientele.

"People come here to get away from all those screens."

To journey into the past, they added, waxing lyrical. I don't know whether they were referring to the supposedly glorious past of the hotel itself or to the more recent but almost more remote period—ten years ago, or twelve now—before "all those screens" arrived.

Cellphones are forbidden, or at least not welcome, in the common areas. And it's true that the guests don't seem the type who would miss them. It's mostly elderly, cultured, badly-dressed English couples that sit on the floral-print sofas in the lounge and on the peeling iron benches in the garden, bestowing their dispirited smiles on everything and everyone around them. They have breakfast early, give a quick nod to the sights surrounding the hotel, and then put their critical gazes out to pasture for hours among the closely shorn privet hedges in the park. They strew shelves and bedside tables with books with unknown authors on their covers, and loud spines. But you know how it is with books like that, especially if they're foreign. Just as with the books' owners, with their incongruous sneakers, they shouldn't be judged by their covers. Sometimes they conceal more than is apparent at first glance.

But we shouldn't overestimate them, either—what both books and owners really bring to mind are wholesome weekly book clubs and pages fastidiously annotated in preparation for the coming debate.

Many of these volumes have been stranded forever on the shelves of the hotel's reading room, unbeatably melancholic. A small library of assorted little tomes is gathering dust there, with all the requisite names in attendance: Maurois; Malraux; Lajos Zilahy; Daphne du Maurier; some mismatched Lawrence Durrells; a few later Hemingways; and of course, level with the floor, scraping the bottom of the barrel down on the lowest shelf, Pearl S. Buck and a Papini that's coming loose from its binding.

And, naturally, there are translations into various languages of the letters and the travelogue of the region that were written by the Scottish poet and illustrious guest from whose stay the hotel squeezes so much value, or at least tries to.

They have his books in a little display case at reception, where they sell them to those guests who haven't brought them from home. I think this must be the poet's busiest sales point in all of Europe; we've all heard of him, but none of us has read him. And with good reason, perhaps: I thought I'd give his little travel journal a go while I was here, and I just couldn't stand it. What little talent he had for badmouthing and insulting the locals. What a misguided series of rhapsodies and clumsy romps with the region's gallants and damsels, almost all of them born of mistakes or deceptions. He was the first tourist to fall into the region's tourist traps, which were set with remarkable speed and intuition as he passed through it. In essentials, they're no better now than they were, to tell the truth.

Why deny it: the hotel itself is a trap. And this is something I think the other guests *do* realize, sufficiently well-traveled or sufficiently British as they are to be able to quickly sniff out any discrepancies between its pretensions to good taste, what it really offers, and the prices it charges. "No, not very good value," my neighbors clucked at their breakfast table this morning. Their murmured conversation was peppered with this phrase—and different variations of it—which was repeated every five minutes like a mantra filled with endless caveats and nuances and scruples, and which served as a spell to lighten the mood. It always cheers us up when we can prove that the thing we so wished to see, what motivated our journey in the first place, was a rip-off.

Meanwhile, the clientele can't be clamoring for the low-to-no-screen diet the hotel keeps us on quite as much as had been claimed at reception. From the very beginning of the day, there's a line to use the single, prehistoric computer that sits in the small, windowless room they are calling a "business center". Only on my third attempt did I manage to actually get a turn at it. It was in use during the siesta that this particular brand of foreign visitors is either unaware of or else feels itself to be above; and it was in use at teatime, when the whitewashed lounges are abuzz—if that's not overstating it—with pre-prandial activity. It was nearly eleven o'clock at night before I could use it, and even then it was only after a lot of throat-clearing—not that my coughs made much of an impression on the deeply concentrated man in shorts, who looked like a retired Bengali cavalryman that had wandered out of an Agatha Christie novel, as he sat in endless contemplation of photos of the sights that awaited him in vain beyond the confines of the hotel.

This business center isn't just squalid, it's positively unhealthy. It takes a while to grow accustomed to the tiny room's stale smell of tobacco (never mind the fact smoking is forbidden, even the garden); it permeates the air, seeming to seep out of the computer itself. It's practically an archaeological specimen at this point; it sends out silky electromagnetic waves like spider webs, which I tried to bat away from my face out of pure reflex.

I visited thehotellife.com, fearing they might have a firewall installed against porn sites. The business center doesn't have a door, and anyone passing by would be able to see the screen. Maybe that's the real firewall. The computer finally connected after an agonizing minute of hesitation. As I had done so many times in these last three days, I typed in the address without looking. Our fingers learn fast.

I moved the cursor arrow to the small keyhole in the padlock that appeared under the page's name. There's an unimposing warning for underage users and those connecting from less permissive countries. The padlock, as always, lit up and widened out to fill the whole screen. The five-second wait becomes more intolerable to me each time, almost insulting.

I entered the password she had given me. I wonder if I'm leaving a trail in the system that she can follow when I do this. I can't tell if I find it exciting or embarrassing that she might know how many times I've visited her page these last few days, and how long I was there each time. And I'm not sure if it's a relief or a disappointment to think that she may never bother to find out, that perhaps this tenuous line of communication between us only exists in my imagination.

Some years ago, the head of an important hotel chain commissioned me to write a prologue for an anthology of hotel-themed stories. They wanted to do a large run and put a copy on all the bedside tables in all the hotels in the chain. The idea wasn't at all bad, and it was certainly less sinister than the Americans with their Bibles; but the guests kept stealing them, and in the end a literal chain came to be used: to tie the spine of each book to a bed leg.

I've forgotten all the stories—and the prologue, of course—except one: a man and a woman, both incurable consumptives en route to their respective sanatoriums, happen to spend one night in a pair of neighboring rooms in a roadside hotel. They never see each other or speak. But they cough and cough all night, and in their feverish, delirious half sleep they find themselves believing they're holding a conversation or singing a duet together through the wall. Their hackings and convulsions are transformed into strains of love and promises of comfort. The next day, the man continues on his way and forgets it all. In her final days in the hospital, the woman can still recall the imaginary duet from that night.

There they were, following my open-sesame: the photos and frozen videos. There are hundreds; I've barely scratched the surface yet. I don't know who Candy, or Steven & Susana, or Dani & Leo are; nor am I familiar with the adventures of *Carnival Day in Rio* or what might have happened on the *White Nights in Saint Petersburg* or on *Bullfight Day in Ronda*. But I already recognize Linda's face and Lewis's body, I know that Jennifer looks younger than she really is and what Joey & Billy did to celebrate their *Thanksgiving with the Twins*. I can reconstruct from memory the decoration—glimpsed only in the background of the videos—of numerous hotel rooms, spectacular suites and tiny cubicles, beach huts, balconies with clinical-looking Jacuzzis, views over the rooftops of hundreds of cities. And the beds—wide beds, narrow beds, round beds, double beds, beds with canopies, water beds, beds surrounded by mirrors; and the wallpapers, stuccowork, trompe l'oeils of varying taste, modernist glass designs, and the alternately dull and sophisticated furniture of room after room scattered all over the globe.

What she said isn't true. Our work isn't similar; in fact, we occupy opposite poles of the profession. I visit hotels, while she's managed to build one immense, labyrinthine hotel out of fragments of thousands of others, tailor made to be just right for her, and just right for anyone. A hotel whose doors are all open, whose rooms are all occupied, a hotel with impeccable service, run with her professional touch, a hotel where one is tempted to stay and live forever.

Sometimes I think I recognize a room in one of her videos or I even seem to remember having found myself between those exact four walls. And then I see a mention of some city I've never visited. So either she's lying, or she's mistaken, or my memory is deceiving me. At least there can be no doubt about the names of the actors: we all take for granted and accept from the start that no one is using their real name.

I moved the cursor down to the bottom of the page and saw what I'd been hoping to see for three days. As though in solidarity, the computer itself seemed to hold its breath: it gave a sort of hiccup and choked down its radioactive whirring. In a newly-appeared thumbnail, right above the name that went with it (Karinne & Leo), I could make out a miniature image of the face of the quick-tempered girl from the room next door, the one who had struggled to put on her shirt as she walked down the hallway at the Imperial and who had insulted me (or had she?) as she passed. I waited a little before clicking on her picture. So—Karinne at last. I had started to think that the woman hadn't managed to "cut anything good from it" in the end (I have just reread and confirmed in my notes that those are the exact words she used that night in my room).

But she had. There was the bad-tempered girl—Karinne, I was supposed to call her Karinne; besides, I didn't have anything else to call her—looking into the camera and wearing exactly the same expression of feigned boredom I had seen on her the first time, on the other side of that cracked door.

I hardly recognized her; she looked prettier than she had at the time. Prettier, or simply more Karinne-like. I couldn't say why or how the photo of this Karinne looked more like Karinne than the girl herself. It wasn't because she looked better in the picture, and it wasn't because the girl I imagined was disappointing in the flesh or because her memory was now permanently tainted by the photograph. It wasn't that—because that always happens, it's a given. People are always disappointing in comparison to their photographs.

I got tired of thinking about it. I'm starting to realize that growing accustomed to the mysteries of her site is so similar to solving them that it's easy to be content with the former alone. I moved the mouse and dragged the cursor over to Karinne's miniature head. The little, white arrow slid along smoothly and silently. It still amazes me, all this deftness in stringing together a series of silent consummations.

It eventually turned into a small hand that I settled over her face like a false nose. To buy some time—for what, I wonder now—I played around with it, touching each eye with the tiny index finger, tracing the outline of her lips with it. I waited a few more moments, and then I clicked.

Many more photos appeared on the screen, the entire series. And the accompanying text: something like a very short story, with just the right dose of a vulgarity that may not have been ironic. It reminded me of the subheads they write for my reviews at the paper—the same forced jocularity, the same robotic, disingenuous goodwill. I refused to write them at first. But eventually I gave in, and sometimes I'll send one in already finished, mimicking their style. It's an act of revenge that they may not even notice and certainly don't mention.

I wonder if she, too, writes her own texts.

It may come as a surprise, but beneath Leo's muscles and angelic face there lies a timid soul. And who would have guessed that the sweet-natured Karinne could get so angry … So this time around, things took a while to heat up between our two new recruits.

It went on to explain that Karinne had just fought with her boyfriend, that Leo had been anxious to play his role well, and that in the end he decided he'd like to perform a solo session. A "session filled with fits and starts," it said, giving no other explanation.

As I read it, I felt like I was back at the Imperial, once again breathing in its carpeted air, which would forever be the perfume of the woman in the next room over. I wonder if that phrase "fits and starts" included me, or if it might even have had me in mind as a possible reader. I liked to think that it was a joke at my expense. She seems like the type who would make them like that: sharpened so finely as to be almost invisible.

I looked at details of the girl's body (she seemed taller again, as she had when I first saw her, in her panties, sitting on the bed): draped over his body; lying on one of his arms, up on her hip; a single hand; a forearm and a dark biceps.

I could also see a corner of the bed, and the beige bedspread on the floor, tangled around the girl's feet. There were photos of scenes reflected in the entryway mirror. The room that could be mentally pieced together from these fragments looked very different from the one I remembered. I changed positions in my seat and waited for the videos to load.

"Good evening."

I'm not sure whether I really jumped in the chair when I heard the voice behind me. But that's how I remember the scene. The cursor, suddenly rebelling at the worst possible moment, took an eternity to obey me, to move to the upper corner and close the window. My heart was pounding, and I must have been either very pale or else blushing brightly when I turned around. Standing in the doorway, smiling at me, was a man I hadn't seen before around the hotel. But his face was familiar. He could have been an unhealthy sixty, or else an enviable seventy. He had a dark silk scarf tied at his neck under a white shirt and a V-neck sweater. All respectable clothes, of course, although their years of wear were evident. I found the scarf disconcerting and even a bit suspicious: a silk scarf around the neck always is. In his case, it exaggerated his get-up almost to the point of looking like the costume of a film director or a hotel manager or even the owner of the whole place. He hadn't stepped into the little room, but he gave the impression of being able to do so without asking permission, of being at all times the legitimate master of or imminent heir to everything around him. In fact, he dressed as the retired Englishmen bumbling around the place ought to have dressed: with the air of an autumnal summer vacationist, inhabiting his role almost to the point of looking misleading.

"They told me at reception that I'd find you here."

He was still smiling, without looking at the computer, which (possibly already too late) was displaying a harmless screen saver with an old sepia- and blue-toned photo of the hotel. It showed the facade overlooking the garden, with a man at the window. At the time, I had no doubt he had seen the porn site perfectly well. Although, thinking it over now, I may be wrong. Rather than tact, his vague look may just have signaled the slightly coy technological confusion that afflicts people at his age.

I was surprised that they should be so well informed at reception of the comings and goings of their guests. They hadn't given that impression, and the lounges and the bar aren't exactly overstaffed with employees keeping tabs on everything. There was an awkward silence. It may only have been awkward for me—he looked unflappable. There was something a little threatening about his sangfroid. In the end, I got up and asked him if he wanted to use the internet.

"No, no, not at all."

I thought this man might be some new breed of hotel detective, charged with keeping a moral eye on the webpages visited within the establishment. Another unlikely profession, of course; but then, I had never looked at porn sites in a hotel before, either.

My first reflex was the guilt of a child caught red-handed. Then I forced myself to adopt the opposite attitude: to defend—like the responsible adult that I am, or that I at least have the right to appear to be—my right to visit whatever sites I like. He spoke before I could say anything.

"I gather you wanted to visit my room."

I moved to sit down again, taken aback. Then utter confusion descended when, as I was taking my seat, I noticed his shoes. Now I think I ought to have examined them the moment I saw him. I always forget to look at people's shoes, and that's a mistake. They save time: they tell us everything.

He wasn't walking around in socks, but he wasn't far from it: he was wearing felt slippers. Perhaps by sheer chance—but perhaps not, and the detail was moving—they matched the scarf around his neck. These slippers were practically from the post-war-era, the backs collapsed inwards by years of use. He must have realized I was looking at them, but he was in no hurry to allay my confusion. That, or he didn't notice it, or else didn't even imagine I could feel any. In the time we spent together, he gave the impression of having forever lost his capacity to feel surprised, as well as the ability to recall or recognize the feeling in others. It transpired he was staying in the famous Scottish poet's room. The truth is, I had completely forgotten I had asked at reception whether I could visit it. When they told me there was someone in it, I didn't want to insist, so I left it at that. I could have pretended I was a student or a devotee of the poet, but the thought of piling another lie on top of all the others that come with this job wearied me.

The man with the scarf explained that he seldom left his room during the day. The receptionists had mentioned my request to him. Usually, he made excuses and wriggled out of it. But this time he felt guilty refusing, knowing how interested I was. If it wasn't too late in the day for me, now was a good time to visit. There wasn't, he wanted to warn me, all that much to see.

I thanked him with more enthusiasm than I really felt. Actually, what I was gladdest at was the idea of getting out of that little cubicle, where every flicker of the screen was an accusing wink. The door to his room opened noiselessly, its hinges as unobtrusive as the low lighting inside. He went in first. He had also gone up ahead of me on the stairs leading to his room. Without turning around to speak, he looked at his key in a way that was strangely self-absorbed—as though he was hostage to a tour guide's routine or to the guilt of the caretaker who exhibits the household's intimate secrets during his masters' absence.

I also looked at his key on the way up. Or rather, at his key ring, which is different from, and more wieldy than the thick, metal medallions that hang by the dozen in the case at reception and give a sinister weight to the keys of the other rooms. They're so heavy that there's something supernatural about them—as though they came from outer space, or were handed down from a lost civilization. All the way to his room, I could feel my own key striking ominously against my thigh.

Before going into the room, I prepared to be confronted with and deflect the shock of another person's privacy. The impression of a head on the pillow; the clothes thrown—or worse, folded—on a chair; the accusing puddle collected in one corner of the bathroom. Details that are twice as painful in other people's hotel rooms, and which I have learned to be ready for.

The texture and scent of the air inside took me by surprise, though: it was complex, and laborious, and although it didn't quite suggest dirtiness, it was saturated with the notes of the most well-lived-in rooms. In the background, the Top 40 were playing very softly on a transistor radio I couldn't locate.

Scents and music all coalesced into a single effusion that pervaded everything: the furniture and the upholstery, my clothes and even my skin. It made me think of all the objects and all the skin, now invisible, that had gone into creating it year upon year. Rather than me invading this man's privacy, in the end it was his unwanted, uninterested, overpowering privacy that invaded me. I forbade myself from attempting to break the strong-smelling air down into its constituent parts. But before I could stop myself, I thought I caught a scent of the depths of childhood and of boiled milk.

And there indeed, on top of a pot-bellied dresser I don't have in my room, were a small electric stove and a milk pan with an off-white rim that I don't have in my room, either.

I could have taken in the room at a single glance, and the little saucepan was really making me want to get out of there that instant. The man gestured toward some armchairs of nobler build than those in my room. As he sat down he announced that, unfortunately, he didn't drink alcohol and so couldn't offer me a nightcap.

It wasn't just the armchairs—the curtains, the headboard on the enormous bed, and the floral wallpaper were all different, too. The man pointed out the desk to me. He remarked without much zeal that it could well be the one the Scottish poet had used. I'm not so sure it's the same furniture as back then, and in fact, I don't think he really believed it, either. But it did obviously belong to an earlier period in the hotel, as though it had escaped various redecorations and general renovations.

Perhaps he saw the doubt in my face. He took a small, framed photo, more yellowing than sepia, down from the wall—an antique print with an undulating, decorative border. It showed the rear facade of the hotel and the recently planted garden: a few puny shrubs overshadowed by a riot of nineteenth-century statuary. There were cheap, painted storks, white plaster busts, and even a little grotto complete with an Our Lady of Fátima. For a second I was gripped by the feeling that I had seen all this before. Then I realized suddenly: it was the same image that had been scanned in for use as the screen saver on the computer downstairs.

"Look, you can see the poet there. It's the only photo of his stay that still exists."

He pointed to the miniscule figure looking out one of the windows. It was so blurry that only with a generous dose of goodwill could you make out the famous goatee beard and goat-like smile: the same ones as on the fronts of the hardcover books they sell at reception. They also preside, in enlarged format, over the breakfast room. It must have been him, although I would hardly say that the beard or the smile were unmistakable—all his contemporaries had that same style and flashed those same teeth.

"Can you see him? He's standing at this very window."

I thought I had done with all that last night. But I confess that today, after breakfast, I went out into the garden with my notebook and sat down on a bench under the rear facade. From here, it isn't hard to locate the window of the room I visited last night: it's the only one that still has curtains with an older print than the rest, and they're still drawn even though it's now eleven thirty. So my night owl host is not an early riser. And in fact, it looks to me as though the window is much further to the right than the one in the photo. Perhaps I don't have such a good photographic memory, perhaps the rooms were bigger in the poet's day, perhaps he was just standing at another window. And now that I think about it, the whole thing with the shepherd children of Fátima was several decades after his stay at this hotel. I ought to cross-check the dates.

But I'll never do that, and I'll never know for sure. It doesn't matter enough to me to find out, nor could it be said to matter in a broader sense, really. It's the same as with the desk the poet supposedly wrote at, the same as with the headboard under which he theoretically rested his little bearded head. It's enough to believe that that was his room, that he wrote his letters at that desk, in order to feel the shiver of recognition, or to feel as though you're feeling it; it's almost the same thing.

I felt it last night, I'll admit, when I saw the photo and thought about how the man and I were just on the inside of that same wall; how the legs and shoes you couldn't see in the photo had, years before, stood at this very windowsill. They were the same legs and shoes that I would have seen if I had sat then in the armchair I was sitting in now.

I thought to myself that that room was similar to the rooms the woman collects for her website: in it, just like on her site, everything that had ever happened was always happening. All down to suggestion, of course. "Well obviously! Just like everything else!" they would have said if they could talk—the photo, the windowsill, the armchair, and everything else in that innumerable army of unflinching things that will never speak, that know nothing other than the eternal present of objects and are oblivious to our obsessive urge to imbue them with a past.

The man with the slippers replaced the photo on the small table that sat between us, then spoke to me with the assumption that I was a great connoisseur of the poet's work. I didn't want to disillusion him.

"I, on the other hand, after all this time living in his room, haven't read a single line of his. And don't think it's out of laziness. Actually, I prefer it this way—it's better I don't find out too much about him. It would be unnerving to feel I was just passing through or that the man might return at any moment to take back what's his. It's silly, I know."

This man had the gift of being quite disconcerting without losing his composure for a second. I asked him how long he was planning on staying.

"Oh, didn't they tell you at reception? I live here."

He had for years, he added, without saying how many. He had come for work, liked the place, and decided to extend his stay. Bit by bit, he had grown accustomed to it, developing routines and arranging with the kitchens for some very simple, very homely meals, developing a taste for the hotel life and its comforts. Like a summary, or an outline, of the life he had lived before.

He had always been, he told me, a man of very little practical sense. Of unprotected tenancy agreements and few possessions and bullyish landlords. Once he had done some calculations and negotiated a bit with the hotel management, he saw it made sense for him to move in. Via a now rickety superstructure of agents and managers, the family that owned the hotel granted his request: lifetime occupancy, at a reasonable price, of the poet's room—which at that time was being kept empty as a sort of miniature museum, with his chamber pot, inkwell, and penholder in small glass cases. The family only asked that he show the historic room to tourists every now and then. The hotel was under financial strain at the time, and this offered them a way to get a reasonable return on the room. With his retirement and a few small annuities on top of it, he could afford to pay the full-pension rate they had negotiated.

"As you will have noticed, I added a few things. And I took away the glass cases, of course. Anyway, that was all a load of junk—all of it fake, or almost all of it. We agreed that this room would be left out of any refurbishments, and I brought in a few bits of furniture that I liked from the others."

I looked again at the saucepan and the little stove in the corner. After listening to him, it seemed to me that those objects, and the general look and even odor of the room—which I couldn't smell any more but which must still have been there, of course—had been transfigured; I felt a new atmosphere, domestic and permanent, solidifying around me. Everything was still in its place, and yet I found myself on the other side of the world from where I thought I had been. I wasn't in the innermost sanctum of the long-dead poet or in a hotel room with a past—I was visiting someone's home.

"And let me tell you, I had to put up a fight to save the wallpaper, even threaten to leave. They were grateful in the end; as you know, people like refurbishing things in this country, but as the years go by they've realized that foreigners have a liking for these things. In time, they'll be glad to have this reminder of what the rest of the hotel used to look like. I often joke that when I'm no longer around, they can turn it into a museum dedicated to me."

Now that I recall the conversation, I'm amazed once again at the ability the man had to offer such dizzying access to his private life without actually revealing more than the outermost fringes of it. I suppose that's what comes of the knack for striking balance that someone who has made a hotel his home would have developed. This man lives day in and day out rooted in the uncertain position of a permanent guest.

He listed the advantages of the arrangement: the newspaper appearing on his doorstep every morning; the flawlessly punctual lunch; the sheets; the daily laundry service and changes of bed linens that he hardly notices any more; and the cleaning ladies' impeccable synchronization with his regular walk and aperitif in the garden. All very tempting, of course, and admirable, up to a point. I thought again of how seductive the idea of becoming an eternal guest at the hotel she has built on her website was—of how easy it would be to spend a whole lifetime exploring all its rooms.

In fact, rather than all these conveniences, what I really envied in this man was the solidity—renewed daily—of his monastic life; the almost unbearable delight of his contemplative retreat, of the life of this hermit who, just like in the famous fairytale, lets decades and centuries pass by while he remains enchanted by birdsong here transmuted into the tinkling of antique reception bells.

A space seemed to open up for me to ask what sort of work he used to do. But as I asked the question, it immediately felt impertinent. Luckily it was forgivable—

he smiled as he got up and walked over to his miniature fridge.

"The kind that these days is called 'creative'."

He leaned over the open door of the fridge and took out an old-fashioned tin.

"Would you like an herbal tea? I always have one at this time of day. It helps me sleep."

On the shelves of the minibar, I glimpsed the proof of what he had told me: some fruit, half a lettuce, and a small plate with the slice of cake that always seemed to be missing from the one that emerged otherwise intact on to the breakfast buffet every morning. At that moment, in that room, they looked positively hallucinatory.

Out of politeness, I ended up accepting an herbal infusion that supposedly had sleep-inducing properties. I who hate infusions. It turned my stomach, and I'm still feeling awkward after being kept awake by it all night.

The man stood side-on by the stove while he waited for the water he'd gotten from the bathroom sink to boil. The feeling that I had seen his face before grew stronger. The place, as I've said, was ideal for suggesting things to the mind, for settling layers of things on top of the things that were already there.

I didn't manage to place him then and I still can't now. The mention of "creative" work set me thinking last night about actors, about artists—of the visual arts or easy-listening varieties. Then I thought about politicians and even athletes of various disciplines whose faces might have graced the front pages in years past. I tried in vain to picture his face projected on the big screen, or under a banner at a rally, or treading the boards, or in front of the cameras at a press conference, or even—eventually—behind a counter. But I felt I was barking up the wrong tree. This morning I've been thinking instead about someone who is famous in a supporting sense, by power of attorney or proxy, someone who has inherited another person's fame, or who processes it and ensures it takes effect.

Perhaps, I thought as we sipped our diffuse infusion, he was a colleague or a predecessor of mine, some forgotten pioneer of hotel criticism. I ought perhaps to have been aware of any legend the trade may have had about some primordial forefather of the country's reviewers, the errant critic who disappeared one fine day and whom I had just run into. Hidden in the most obvious place, where, for that very reason, it would never occur to anyone to look for him. Living out his old age in an ageing hotel.

It would have been crass to insist, to let slip a banal "I think I've seen you somewhere before." The steam from the hot water was reincarnated as a wistful fog on the windowpanes. Partly to banish the tepid triviality of the tea, partly to break the silence that was apparently only uncomfortable for me, and partly to see if I could inspire his sense of trust and coax him into solving the mystery, I decided to confess my own.

I explained my reasons for being in the hotel and for wanting to see his room. For the second time in less than a week, I broke the anonymity that I had so strictly maintained up to now. And both times with complete strangers. Or almost. The truth is, I wouldn't know where on the scale of mutual unacquaintance I should place individuals who are united by a connection that may be the most tenuous one imaginable beyond, or this side of, being total strangers: that of being hotel-room neighbors.

In this case, we didn't even share a dividing wall. And unlike my neighbor at the Imperial, he didn't recognize my name or remember ever having read my column. And he certainly did not reveal himself to be a colleague or the original master critic.

He smiled without looking at me and blew unnecessarily into his tea, which by then must have been as horribly lukewarm as mine. Then all of a sudden he looked up, listened intently, and gestured for me to be quiet. Neither of us spoke for a moment, and I listened again to the background drone of some inconsequential, formulaic song coming out of the hidden radio.

Then he looked at me with a sly smile.

"How odd. They've played the same song twice in a row. Did you notice?"

I hadn't, of course. The music had caught my attention as I came in (well, only relatively—there's nothing strange about a person leaving a radio on when they step out of a room, or always having it on for background noise and company), and then I had tuned it out, lost the musical thread of the songs—in the same way that I no longer noticed the room's peculiar smell now that I was immersed in it. I was taken aback to discover that the man had only been paying as much attention to my visit as he had to what was on the radio.

"No, actually, I can't say that I did."

The man looked at me as he replied.

"Well they did, they just played this one."

The two of us were quiet again, and then, in the middle of the chorus, the song was cut off. Suddenly there was total silence; we looked at each other and I shuddered. You never hear silence on a radio, I thought.

It felt as though it would last forever, as though we would remain this way eternally: still and quiet, all our attention on the silent radio. Then there was the sound of someone clearing his throat, and a thud, and a new song started playing. I think they skipped a few slots, because over the melody there came a brusque voice, devoid of the usual pomp, to announce the Number One of the week.

The man with the slippers let out a little laugh.

"How funny. The presenter must have fallen asleep."

Then he swilled his tea around, took one last sip, left the cup on the table, and spoke to me again.

"Ah. What an enjoyable job. And a difficult one, too, I take it?"

It took me a moment to realize he was taking up again the conversation that had been interrupted by the radio.

"Well, I'm even gladder I invited you up here, then. Do me the kindness of giving the place a good write-up. It might help them keep it open. What would I do if they closed it? Just think of it—where would I go now?"

I don't know what time it was when I left his room, but when I drew the curtains in my own, the morning was already limping into the counterfeit spring that had managed, with its amateur trickery, to get me out into the garden. I spent hours tossing and turning in the bed and getting nowhere. And now, though the sun may be shining, I can feel on my back, through my sweater, the thin, chill wind that the Scottish poet complained about so bitterly, gifted as he was at glossing even the slightest current of air.

Because before going back to my room last night, I stopped by the internet alcove again. I walked down the silent hallways, lit only by the slivers of light under the doors of the unexpectedly nocturnal English guests. I crossed the ground-floor lounges, which were vast in a way they hadn't appeared during the day and frozen with a disapproving air in the orange light of the garden lamps streaming in through the windows. I turned on the light in that tiny computer room, then turned on the computer, praying that the stupid startup sound wouldn't disturb the slumber of the night receptionist in his armchair behind the counter. Or that of the hotel itself (which I could feel wheezing around me through the lungs of all the guests heaving in unison), exhausted after a hundred years of uninterrupted watchkeeping and service.

At last, I was able to open the video they shot at the Imperial. Without the sound, it seemed even more furtive—this enhanced, improved replay of the things I had seen, and the things I had only imagined, the other night in the other hotel. Once again, I felt like I was spying on them from the other side of the door. But instead of through a crack, now it was as though I were seeing the girl and boy through an imaginary keyhole, positioned perfectly to take in the whole scene. I saw how the bed came to be unmade, why the mattress had ended up bare. There was nothing much worth seeing, nothing I hadn't seen before. Nothing I would have wanted to see, in any case: the real mysteries that this scene only pretended to resolve. I didn't see the boy having trouble getting turned on, I couldn't smell the hostile new carpet, I couldn't feel the chill of the room or hear the rain falling beyond the windowpanes. In this little movie, everything seemed sunny and simple. It took an enigma and exchanged it for a hackneyed, old riddle.

I saw no trace of old Pedro in the video. And caught no sight of her, of course. There was no hint of her presence in the whole video. In fact, it had been shot in such a way as to banish the idea that she was present or even existed. Except, that is, for the indelible trace of the shoot itself: her indispensable camera, and her eye that had witnessed the whole scene through it. That was something you had to make an effort to remember, and that I would have forgotten, myself, in other circumstances: if her face and her conversation were not so present in my mind, if I were not able to summon up so clearly—as I'm doing now—all her gestures and words, her exact tone of voice, her technical instructions.

I saw, in the end, what she had seen. Or rather, what she wanted me—and thousands of other subscribers—to see. Every fold, every face, every position. And yet, when the video finished, I felt disappointed. She had found the perfect hiding place.

I don't know how long I sat there looking at the frozen image on the site's main page. It was a while before I noticed a red button with white lettering:

Our Itinerary

I probably hadn't seen it until then precisely because it was so obvious: it was in a prominent position on the screen, next to the box where subscribers enter their username and password. This woman has clearly mastered the art of hiding things in plain view. A new window opened when I clicked on it.

Below are the cities we will be visiting in the coming month. If you live in one of them and are interested in working with us, don't hesitate to write us. Please attach three recent photos, and remember that you will be required to provide at least two forms of ID at your interview in order to confirm that you are eighteen or over.

A list of cities followed, with their respective dates. It was an erratic route, at least at first glance. If you joined the dots on a map, it would seem to trace the mark of a particularly cunning Zorro, a scrawl with no discernible hand or intention behind it. Perhaps she doesn't have either.

I copied the list onto a separate slip of paper and stuck it between the pages of this notebook before going to sleep. I've got it here beside me now, on the table—the names of six cities under the hotel's sad, blue letterhead of this hotel that prices so high its writing paper with a pedigree. I had to weigh it down with a rock from the garden so that it wouldn't blow away. Actually, it wouldn't matter if it flew off on the wind or miraculously burst into flames this very instant. I realized this morning that at some point in the middle of the night—in the half sleep of warped ideas that I've forgotten but that must have been stored in some adjacent room in my mind—I had learned it by heart.

My host from last night has just appeared at his window. He opened the curtains and is now leaning out on the windowsill, as though to mimic the position of the blurry poet in his yellowing photo. Right now, I might be in the position of the person who, a hundred years ago, trained his lens on him from below and bore eternal witness (dubiously, but indelibly) to his stay here. It's past twelve o'clock. He is not an early riser. And why would he be? They'll be waiting for him punctually with his out-of-hours breakfast, and with everything else, too. Everything contained in the tiny world of this hotel will adapt to his rhythms and his desires, all day long and on every identical day that follows. Everything will happen according to his schedule. He is the master of his time here, and holds more sway over things as a guest than any owner could.

"Good morning!" he shouted down to me. Scottish readers gave us disgruntled looks from the neighboring garden benches. The very wind was like a librarian's shushing.

He asked me if I wanted to wait for him down in the garden to have an aperitif at one o'clock. It was a pleasant, tempting offer. The aperitif to a pleasant and tempting life, perhaps, in which it would always be cocktail hour in this autumnal garden, and in the endless autumns that followed. I would spend my days ensconced under the window of this poet, this fake, efficient acting-god of the establishment. And at night, again as a perpetual guest, I would return punctually to that other hotel, her hotel. I noticed a last aftertaste in my mouth of that useless brew the man gave me to drink last night.

I returned his greeting loudly, happy to irritate the English guests and happy, too, in the euphoric knowledge that I was only passing through. Enjoying the prospect of the pleasure in departing of he who departs, the joy of suddenly finding myself with a ready-made itinerary that will allow me to vacate this bogusly British establishment without so much as a farewell.

"Thanks, but I can't. I'm just leaving."

Of course, when it comes to hotels, every departure is made without a farewell. It's true that their rooms and closets submit willingly to the pleasure of being filled. Their shelves and drawers welcome the symbols of our existence, and our shirts flap on their coat hangers like flags over effortlessly conquered islands. But she was right: traveling with a purpose changes everything. The thrill of occupying a virginal room seems pale to me now next to the joy of vacating one and the converse delight of leaving without looking back—of packing up, glancing at the map, and going.

The Hotel Life

This week our critic draws out his summer with an off-season trip to the seaside. Should we be taking advantage of the autumn offers at the Royal Marina Hotel and getting one over on the calendar? We'll leave it to you to decide.

THE LOW SEASON

Do you recall that a few years ago I reviewed the Royal Marina for a special summer issue? Well, they don't at the hotel, where the staff do not seem to recognize me (I do recognize them; as you know, I have a photographic memory when it comes to a good receptionist). On my return, at first glance at least, I can report that little has changed. Except for the season—which, in this sort of hotel, changes everything. No difficulty this time in getting a room with a view of the sea. Too much of a view, perhaps, and too much sea—the damp reaches up as far as the floor I'm on, and as I write, a stiff, autumnal tide has just swallowed up the beach below the promontory.

The room is long on antiquated comforts and short on modern conveniences. In its heyday, this place was the last word

*in choice summer holiday destinations for the chic. It reminds
me a little of the hotel I wrote to you from a week ago. Except
that, for now, the damp air of the Marina carries no whiff of
imminent bankruptcy or closure. It sits atop its hill with its
slate-roofed dormers, its overelaborate balconies, with its miserly
exterior touch-ups in various shades of white, and with no
castle or cathedral to compete with—the sturdiest monument in
this city with a hotelier's soul that would balk at the slightest
change. The sea and the port have never managed to awaken in
it a spirit of adventure.*

*When the time comes for an overhaul, it will be met with
obliging town councilors, swiftly granted permits, and local
philanthropists. An extra word—"spa" or "resort"—will
be appended to the proud sign over the front door. There will be
much re-tiling of bathrooms.*

*The cost-cutting and foot-dragging in the actual
implementation of it all will be born, in this case, out of the
respectable inertia that rules over all life in the city. And of the
dependence on routine of a clientele who would be most put out
to return for the nth summer to find everything out of place, the
radiators refitted, the drafts and a thousand other discomforts
that provide such good conversational fodder disappeared.*

*This was not, in the beginning, a hotel without ambition.
But the pretension that remains is all inherited. All the rough
edges and all the shrillness have been polished away by the same
hundred years of use that have left every step worn smooth and
all the upholstery faded. Take a close look if you stay here—
there is nothing in this hotel that on closer inspection does not
reveal itself as mended, patched, repainted, or repaired. In the
shadows behind the gilding and the stucco, it's superglue and
3-IN-ONE that truly reign in the Royal Marina.*

128

Some will be depressed by this fondness for the quick fix.
I liked it on my first visit, actually—this discreet, domestic,
tumbledown feel. That summer, I would often walk among
the unruly hydrangeas in the garden. Weeds pushed
through the gaps in the fence. There were card games afoot; you
could hear the bouncing of tennis balls, and splashing in the
ridiculously deep swimming pool. On this second visit, however,
I haven't set foot there. The tables and chairs are stacked under
green tarps, the lawn is permanently damp and I don't have
any sensible shoes.

The empty lounges and the hallways smell like some
antique cleaning product, some pine spray discontinued long ago
and taken, perhaps, from some magnificent reserve piled up in
the basement. They gave me a half-price room that's taller than
it is wide, with unreachably high moldings and a bay window
overlooking the beach. The moisture and the salty air seep in
through the cracks. Every morning, the furniture is covered in
a fine, white dust that tastes of the sea and medicine, and I've
gotten into the habit of running my finger along the backs of
the chairs and bringing the salt to my lips during the downtime
I spend in the room.

There weren't many of those, though, as every wasted
minute I spent far from her, or from the possibility of
finding her, pained me. I arrived in that city—the first
on her list—when, according to her dates, she would
already be getting ready to leave again. It was going to
be difficult to find her, and I almost preferred it that way.
I wasn't expecting to catch up with her right away, and
deep down, I would have felt awkward if I had. Maybe
more than she would.

It was getting dark early, there were intermittent showers, and the sun shone only in short spells, never enough to dry the sidewalks or warm the air. I checked into the Royal Marina confidently—my review from three years ago could well have steered her there. In the end, it felt more forgivable to be following her trail if she thought that she was in fact following mine.

I didn't ask for her at reception; I dreaded the tired, old lecture about respecting clients' privacy and feared the staff would put her on the alert. And besides, what exactly could I ask them if all I knew was that she was tall and elegant and about forty? All the same, for a few days it felt as though I was about to run into her any moment in the lobby or in the dining room, around every hallway corner. Whenever I used the elevator, I would get nervous as the doors opened. I would prepare myself, compose my face. But there would be no one there: just an empty hallway or the dull, stale air of the lobby.

At first, I made sure to spend time in the different lounges in the hotel. Later, when it was clear that she never went into them, I took to walking along the streets that ran parallel to the line of beaches and boulders where that side of the city ended. I snooped around a few other possible hotels. Perhaps she had chosen not to follow my recommendation about the Royal Marina after all. Perhaps because it was expensive, or because it was uncomfortable, or impractical; whatever the reason, I didn't want to include among the several possibilities the fact that she might be avoiding me. In reality, she couldn't have guessed I would be there. Much less that I was following her.

Even I hadn't completely admitted to myself that that's what I was doing. On the contrary: while I was at the Marina, I tried to anticipate her and her tastes, to go over to her side, to focus on things in the way I imagined she would have chosen to frame them. As I left my room each morning, I would set to work and assume the task of being her; after tracing her possible routes on foot, I would return to my room every evening convinced that I knew her a little better.

It took me a while to realize that this way of being in the city, of seeing it through her eyes, was a new variation on a secret game I had made up for myself during my boyhood as an only child. I called it (or perhaps I never called it anything at the time and the name became attached to the memory later, in some particular moment I have now forgotten) "The Road to the Gallows." It must have sprung from inappropriate things I'd read or violent films I almost certainly shouldn't have been watching. The game was simple: it consisted of imagining that I was looking at everything around me for the last time. In convincing myself that the tedious walk to school or the long trek to the park or the bus ride to run some errand was in fact my last journey, that I was a condemned man on the way to his execution.

It allowed me to use that gift all children have for boundless self-pity—and the children who have it in greatest measure are the know-it-alls who learn to see everything, including themselves, through misunderstood books. Given the humble simplicity of the game's methods, the power of their effects never ceased to amaze me. I had only to decide that the game was underway, I had only to force myself to imagine that I would never again turn this corner or pass this shop front or greet this shopkeeper for the unremarkable corner or drab shop front to be transformed into a thing of transcendental importance. The day-to-day scenery, the familiar sequence of side streets and tree beds, immediately became painfully real, burned into my retina. I had no compunction—children don't—about mustering the sentimentality necessary to work myself up to the point of tears. Farewell, streets! Farewell, doors and doormen! This was the last time—truly, *the very last!*—that I would see these sights I knew so well. The most wonderful thing about the pretense was that, for just a second, as the game came to its silent, secret climax, they became things I was seeing for the first time.

En route to the imagined gallows, I was the listener to whom I told my own stories, the audience for whom I filmed and projected my impressions. It occurs to me now that my present pursuit might be a more complicated variant of that same game, made up by a more complicated variant of the same child, who is tired of creating his own fun and has ended up looking for other companionship.

There were a lot of hotels in the city. I could reject most of them at a glance. They were too private, or they were too indiscreet. With their miniature gardens and their ten or fifteen bedrooms, they imitated the capacious summerhouses that the *haute bourgeoisie* of the drier provinces built in the area a hundred years ago. They imitated them, or else just inhabited them; many of those pretentious chalets—which the owners, in their day, called *hôtels* even though they were private houses, adopting the French sense of the word (the term "chalets" wasn't yet in use)—had not survived the divvying-up of the inheritance handed down from the founding patrician. They had been sold off in a hurry and converted into real hotels at last, in an unusual display of etymological justice.

The bourgeoisie's tastes had changed, too. Or maybe they were just never as *haute* again after that. A lot of the houses had been demolished and now found their plots occupied by apartment blocks, their paint corroded by sea-spray, their ground floors lined with woeful shops selling beach gear.

For my part, I hardly went to the beach. She would have found it depressing: the permanently wet sand, the bland sea, the waves bashing uselessly against the rocks. It did offer the strategic advantage of excellent visibility for hundreds of yards in every direction, in spite of the haziness brought on by the afternoon mist. But I never saw her there. Just the retirees who walked the whole length of the beach at low tide, their pant legs rolled up and their feet purple with cold.

Gradually, I withdrew toward the center of town, far from the summer vacation district with its empty streets and small, boarded-up chalets. Because there was also a wintertime city, which pretended to believe it sat hundreds of miles from the coast. The natives there were very careful to look down their noses at the beach. Only very rarely would they set foot on the promenade (and never before dusk), and they always wore long sleeves, even in August. I remembered that right from my first visit, their limpid pallor and their habit of burying themselves in cardigans and scarves in the middle of June made them easy to tell apart from the out-of-towners with their bare-chested tans.

The downtown was neither pretty nor ugly. I felt suddenly wearied by everything again: the verdant, preened park; the dazzling, bustling cafes at teatime; the hours forming lumps as they drained slowly away through a city that knew it had nothing to offer in the low season and was rallying itself for winter. I didn't allow myself to be taken in by all this pretense of collective resignation: I knew as well as the inhabitants themselves that even in summer, no beach or boulevard can throw off the veil of primness that has smothered them every single day of the last hundred years, since the supposedly glorious era of those long summer holidays enjoyed by the great and the good.

I would go back to the hotel as night was beginning to fall. At about the time the streetlights were turning on, a dampness would drift in off the sea and turn to mist. One only noticed it on finding that his jacket was wet through, or when a droplet of water, having condensed in secret, would creep gently down his cheek.

There was just one nice afternoon. At the last minute, the eternal clouds parted and the sun came out and spread its warmth like a guest arriving late with breathless excuses. I started to feel itchy under my sweater. The streetlights turned on in spite of themselves and shone uselessly in the warm air. Even I felt annoyed, practically offended. When the good weather reached me, I had already changed tack and was reluctant to take my coat off. The idea of going back to the hotel and shutting myself away in my room was awful. And I couldn't count on the cafés, either, because I could see from the street that they were now empty—their customers were drifting with seeming nonchalance down discreet side streets toward the promenade, alone or in little groups, all of them pretending they weren't on their way to watch the sun set over the sea. Unseasonable sparrows chirped on the sidewalks and the sand lining the tree beds dried out. It all made the possibility of finding her feel slimmer.

I was in a bad mood now, and as a last resort, I walked into a movie theater. The girl at the box office warned me that the show had started half an hour earlier. I hadn't even checked what the movie was. I just wanted to take refuge in the darkened room, then come out and be met by the autumn night.

Like the hotel and the whole city, the movie theater was putting off remodeling for now; the moment for it to be chopped up into a multiplex was still to come. In the hospital-green lobby hung posters for unconvincing movies. It smelled of the shriveled chocolate bars at the snack counter, and a toilet cistern dripped. I felt better. There was no sign of an usher; I ducked into the din of explosions and screams coming from the theater.

There weren't many people, so I could choose my seat. It's true that it was already half an hour into the movie, but it was all designed so that you could glean everything you needed five minutes before the end. That was fine with me, too, and I would have disengaged completely from what was happening on the screen—an underwater car that could also fly, people who would die upon seeing a certain photo—if it hadn't been for a group of kids only slightly less adolescent than their clothing. They came in making a ruckus and stumbling all over each other and laughing.

They sat in the row in front of me. The tallest one wore a cap whose visor blocked the part of the screen where things were happening. He had borrowed the style from movies like this one, and he was getting past the age for wearing it. A girl next to him wouldn't stop chewing gum, and she kept squealing when he tickled her.

I noticed the fighting spirit that is sometimes awakened in me in movie theaters, and even a sudden interest in the fortunes of the space car. I made my seat creak, I sighed, I cleared my throat, I coughed and even shushed a few times; the tickling, smacking kisses, and giggling were redoubled. I ended up leaning forward to ask the kid to change seats or to take off his hat.

I had assumed he was expecting a confrontation, if not provoking one. But in fact, he jumped in his seat and turned around with genuine surprise. I gave an even bigger start myself—by the light of the screen, I could make out the logo of thehotellife.com, which by then I could have drawn from memory, on the visor of his cap. We held each other's gaze for a moment. Without a word of complaint, the boy—worthy son of a city sworn to not frightening off outsiders—took off his hat. I sank quietly back into my seat.

At the Imperial, she had spoken to me about "merchandising" (and not ironically, by the way), about hats and T-shirts. But not about how you could get ahold of them. Would they be on sale in normal shops? Perhaps thehotellife.com had an online shop that I had overlooked. I doubted it—by now I really did know all of the website's hidden little corners like the back of my hand.

Perhaps she gave them out herself to her actors, or raffled them off to her subscribers. The group of kids started to forget about me again, or else to grow bolder. I stayed very still in my seat, breathing deeply to calm the thumping in my chest that was becoming almost painful, preparing myself for the moment when the lights would go up.

The movie took forever to find an ending. While the room was still in darkness, the whole gang leapt out of their seats and charged toward the emergency exit. I ran after them. When I came out into the hallway I nearly collided face-on with the kid in the cap and his girlfriend, who had fallen behind the rest and were transfixed by something on a cellphone.

The two of them looked up at me, the smiles, like those of new parents, that they had bestowed on the telephone still on their faces. I asked if could I ask them something. The boy became serious and the girl laughed. They weren't going to make things easy for me.

I mentioned the hat and motioned with my chin toward his forehead. The boy wasn't wearing the hat any more, but out of sheer habit he also looked for it with his eyes. Even the girl looked up at his hair for a second. Then they looked back at me, their faces just as indifferent as before, although not exactly hostile; it's rather that they were stunned, their reflexes still dulled from all those screens.

Eventually, they reacted. The boy laughed and the girl became very serious.

"My hat?"

He laughed again, and the girl joined in with him this time. Meanwhile, there was no trace of the hat; he wasn't carrying it in his hand, and it wasn't sticking out of any of his pockets.

"She gave it to me."

He cocked his chin toward her, laughing. The girl pretended to be surprised. There was nothing for it. They improvised a little mock-fight on the spot, complete with jeers and insults. After a while, she pretended to remember they had an audience. She adopted a serious tone to answer me.

"I don't know what hat you mean."

I wanted to see this thing through to the end. I could already visualize my anger and the long night in my hotel room. I told them it was important, and even I thought I sounded crazy. Out in the street, the others were whistling and bent over laughing. The boy and girl glanced over sideways at them and caught the contagious laughter as they rushed out to the sidewalk.

I also walked out into the street, but slowly. I was comforted to see that night had fallen. It was misty again, and the walk back to the hotel wasn't so awful anymore. I decided that, rather than having been a missed opportunity, this augured well, it was a sign that I was on the right track. I remembered what she had told me about the years of effort it had taken her to perfect her technique for approaching people. I wanted to take this misstep as she would surely have taken it: sportingly. I would also have to start learning to polish my technique. In the end, it's all part of the job.

For the first time in all these years, the people at the paper refused to publish a review of mine. They didn't want the one about the Royal Marina; it wasn't long ago that they ran the last one, and there's no need to revisit it for now. They're right, of course. To get around it, they're going to put out a write-up of an airport hotel I didn't even remember I'd sent them, and which they had been keeping "on ice", as they put it, in case something unexpected happened.

"You know, in the minibar."

They made their placatory joke but couldn't help emphasizing this "unexpected" side of it all, and the question of exactly what kind of unexpected situation this was hung in the air, and underlying it, the question of what on earth I was up to. They never quite formulated it, and I didn't feel obliged to answer.

Something they did ask is what next week's hotel would be. I said I'd call them to let them know. But I may not. In this second city on her list, there aren't any of interest, as far as I know. In fact, there are only two that are even acceptable; the first is this one, the

141

Central Hotel, where I decided to stay. It's like the city it stands in: proper, predictable, neither very small nor especially large; as central and bland as its name suggests, less functional than it looks, and not even dull enough to lay claim to its own special brand of mystery. The other hotel is just across the road. That is practically the only way in which it is different. It's also its great advantage: from the window of my room I can see all the windows on the facade across the street, and I have a commanding view of the main entrance. It's like staying in both for the price of one. If I can keep watch patiently and methodically, it shouldn't be too difficult to find out for certain if she's staying in one or the other.

I have no idea what could have brought her here. I arrived on the date specified on her page. I'd spent the evening before the journey in the Central Station of the previous city, in case she had decided to go by sleeper train. I looked up the timetables, arrived with time to spare, and pretended to say goodbye to someone from the platform while I made a check of the near-empty compartments. I looked closely at the passengers getting on the train and hurrying between the carriages. If I had seen her on that train, I would have jumped aboard with nothing more than what I had on me. If I had had to pay a fine to the ticket collector, I would have paid it; I would have bought what I needed for a few nights and called the hotel and had them send my luggage on. It's in these senseless practical arrangements that my days trickle away.

I'm dividing my time between the two hotels, and repeating across lounges, lobbies, bars, and dining rooms the stalking ritual that I've been perfecting lately. With the help of some tips and sidelong glances, I have secured the most strategic tables and armchairs: the ones with views of the elevators, counters, phone booths, and revolving doors. I scarcely go out into the street. We're further to the north now, and the rain is relentless; all the hoods and umbrellas will make it difficult to pick her out. Some mornings, after breakfast, I return to my room. Stretched out on the bed, I listen to the silence of the hotel, which is punctuated by the gurgling of draining bathtubs. When I can't endure it any longer, I put on my coat and go out onto the balcony. I lean against the railing, and the hours slip by.

I may not have seen her, but I've seen a lot of other things—more than I would ever have hoped to see from the rooftop of our house when I was a boy. Every morning, a couple of night owls return to the hotel across the street and go up to their room, which is at the same height as mine. Their dreary faces appear at the windows as they draw the curtains, which stay closed all day. They only open again when the couple, with renewed good cheer, emerge onto their balcony in their bathrobes. It looks like the endless rain lifts their spirits, and that endears them to me. Behind them, I can see their unmade bed and a couple of suitcases open on the armchairs. They move around the room for a while, drying their hair and buttoning up their clothes, and in the corner of the bedroom that I can see, the orange glow from the bedside lamps gives a tantalizing promise of pleasures to come. They only go out when it's very late, after going back to the room again for a hundred things they've forgotten. Two nights ago, as I watched them leaving their hotel, I saw that their journey was short: without so much as opening their umbrella, they crossed the street and walked into this one. I deliberately got up early the next day and found them eating breakfast at a table near mine. I ran up to my balcony to check that, a short while later, they really did retrace their steps back to the other hotel. Behind their backs, the two doormen gestured to each other from opposite sidewalks.

They're my favorite guests, and every morning I'm afraid they won't show up and draw their curtains. I like to know that they're tucked up in their hotel during the day, and at night it comforts me to watch over their sleep in one of the rooms in mine.

At about the time they fall asleep, in the room next door to theirs, a child sharing the room with his parents starts bouncing up and down on his extra bed; he forces them to keep the cartoon channel switched on at all times and to steal kisses on the balcony in the rare moments he isn't watching. In another, one floor up, a very well-dressed woman changed her earrings five times in front of the mirror one night, only to end up not leaving the room and disappearing the next morning, replaced by an endless succession of colorless guests with the defeated look of people getting off a long, overnight flight.

On the second floor is a middle-aged man who looks like a soap opera heartthrob and who will usually eat his breakfast—dissecting kiwis, drinking cup after cup of coffee in small sips—while talking on the phone. He has a range of glass bottles on the dresser and an army of suits in the closet. He leaves it wide open for the duration of the half hour or more it takes him to choose his clothes in the morning. By the time he goes out on to the street, a car is waiting for him. His chauffeur is either inspired by, or else inheriting, his ties.

In the middle of the morning, when the rooms are empty, a battalion of cleaning ladies arrives. At exactly the same moment, I can hear some bustling around in the neighboring rooms of my own hotel. They empty waste paper baskets and throw windows open, tidy everything in a flash; they debate whether or not to change sheets only used once, and sometimes decide not to. They greet each other with shrieks of laughter from one balcony to another, as they shake out the doormats and unceremoniously stir up the domestic atmosphere that has stagnated in each room—shaking it out, dusting it off, sweeping it away, rubbing it down, besprinkling it with their endless sprays—until it has no other choice but to retreat into the corners of the closets, into the very last dresser drawers where sometimes, by some miracle, a single shoetree, a book with a page marked, a restaurant card with a phone number scribbled on it, or an empty contact lens case has escaped the purge. Things like the ones I have found in the drawers in this room, and other rooms before it. Things that I now regret not having collected; they could testify to a whole hotel life that's starting to feel like a long dream or a parenthesis pointlessly dragged out.

145

The other day, I came back to my room after breakfast to find one of the cleaning women, in her uniform, humming to herself as she changed my sheets. We both gave a nervous smile and then, like players in a music-hall sketch, both started to withdraw at the same time. After a pantomime of aborted interjections and reciprocal goodwill, I ended up leaving her by herself in my room. I can't quite work out who was violating the privacy of whom.

One day, in the middle of the afternoon, a well-dressed man walked into one of the rooms and took possession of the place with a series of movements that spoke of years of experience. He opened the window by a very precise fraction, plugged in his laptop, and poured himself a drink from the minibar. He tested the lights and the box spring; he turned the television on, flicked through the channels without pausing on a single one, and turned it off again; he hung up a freshly-ironed shirt that was brought in to him.

Then he sat down to write. And then he did nothing. He kept staring at the computer screen, sipping his drink while the room grew dark around him and was eventually swallowed up in the glow of the laptop. I was moved by his expertise in solitude. His gestures reminded me of my own.

But I can also see the future from my room; I need only go out onto my balcony, which sits on the canted corner of the facade. The main entrance is five floors below me. And so it is I, before anyone else, who sees the free taxi coming up the side street to where the guests are waiting, weighed down with luggage; or the tour guide, running late, whose entire group has grown impatient to get out and visit the unlikely monuments that this city does conceal, after all; or the pair of secret, ante meridiem lovers, with a liking for novel-like arrangements, who, having agreed to arrive separately and wait for each other in the room, have been too punctual and have to pretend they don't know each other as they run smack into one another at the front door of the hotel.

You need only a little patience—at times a surprisingly small amount of patience—to see those same couples part again at the door without saying goodbye. Like a wizard gazing into his crystal ball, I can see very clearly what happens next, and predict what will happen in the end—the way one or the other or both of them, on turning their corner, will cry dejectedly or light a cigarette or whistle or talk into their cellphone or look at their watch and break into a run as they forget the hotel and the room they're leaving behind and everything that happened there.

I've been perfecting my powers, sharpening my sight. Even at night, in the light of the streetlamps reflected in the puddles, I can see what's to come: the unconvincing bachelors from the personal ads will arrive alone, carnation in a buttonhole and newspaper in hand, and they will loiter around the door and end up either leaving or plucking up the courage to go in, and come out again either alone or paired up with someone five minutes or five hours later; the couples that kiss and pat each other on the back at the beginning of the evening and by the end of their dinner, before the others are even out of sight, are already badmouthing them with a venom whose vapors will reach all the way up to me here on the fifth floor.

And then, some bitter afternoons, I only see the present. The city absorbed in its rhythmic purr, the people coming and going like something out of an illustrated schoolbook: the grocer at his fruit stand, the builder with his bricks, the fancy lady looking at her reflection in the shop windows, the security guard with his nightstick. You can almost even see the young boy with a tray of buns balanced on his head who's always crossing the street in one corner at the very back of all old photographs. I see myself in this tableau, too, of course—the man standing on the balcony with nothing to do, the character of no discernible profession or apparent contribution to anything, who fills a gap, and whom the teachers leave out of their explanations.

It's more and more difficult, yes, but I still step out on to the street when I get tired of wandering along the hallways or whiling away the hours in the lounge, of looking out the window and hoping that, any moment, it will be her I see coming around the corner or getting out of a taxi or opening the curtains in a room in the hotel across the way. I go to a nearby café and kill time reading the local papers and keeping an eye on the passersby outside the window. I'm served by a waitress who looks just the type to appear on thehotellife.com. If she had seen her, she would have taken her on. The café is centrally located and very well known; everyone visiting the city ends up stopping in. And in fact, after a couple of days, I came to convince myself that she had already done just that.

In a place like this, four mornings are enough to make you a regular. By dint of sitting at the same table, giving good tips, and turning out a few obvious jokes, I had struck up a rapport with the waitress. Today, on the fifth day, during her lunch break, I waited for her in the corner of the café and we went upstairs to my room. She didn't want the other waiters to see her with me, but she said hello to the hotel receptionists as we went past the counter.

I asked her if she'd ever posed for thehotellife. com, shortly after we'd gone into the room, as she was unbuttoning her blouse. She had already taken her skirt off, and I could see the mark its metal clasp had left, like the negative of a tattoo: white with pink edges. I had planned to ask her some time later, to take advantage of the ten extra minutes before she would have to go back to work, a time when people often reveal truths to each other, or at least allow each other a little license to make them up. But I think I read too much into her breeziness in greeting the receptionists. I thought I could catch her when her guard was down and her back turned, take advantage of the weak flank her awkward position presented. I tried to ask her in the same way my neighbor from the Imperial would have, imitating more or less the tone in which she'd spoken about her job that night.

She whipped around sharply, still sitting on the edge of the bed. She stopped unbuttoning. She didn't need to

149

understand the question to comprehend the tone of it perfectly—she sensed a trap. I got tangled up in pathetic explanations. She stayed very still, her hands still under her shirt, looking at me without listening, resolved either to not hear any of it or to appear not to. Then, scoffing, she struggled to get the loose clasp on her skirt closed again. She thought (or wanted to make me think she thought) that it was I who was proposing she appear in a video. She insulted me without raising her voice, and I have to give her credit for achieving an effect that was both icy and long-lasting—I'm still feeling the shivers from her final "what's your problem, freak." She did slam the door as she left, though.

I won't be able to go back to the café, of course. And coming down to the dining room for dinner, I get the feeling the receptionists and even the waiter are giving me dirty looks.

It turns out the city of the twin hotels still had one particularly low blow in store for me. Tonight, before getting on this train to the next city, I found a new entry on her page that had been posted recently. In the photos, I recognized with near terror the worn upholstery of the sofa, the whitish wood of the headboard, the tiles in the background of a rather well executed shower scene in one of the unmistakable bathrooms of the Royal Marina.

I deserve that, I forced myself to think and almost say out loud. I've looked for her without entirely believing I would find her. I've followed her without ever letting go, I now realize, of a last scrap of irony that might allow me to save face, even if only in front of myself. As though I had agreed to join in some pastime, some board game for grown-ups, that had no strings attached and that didn't make me look silly in my own eyes.

Or, most importantly, in hers—sometimes, in the street or in a bar, I would turn around suddenly, convinced I was going to catch her watching me. More than once, as I walked out of a shop or turned a corner, I thought I saw her in the distance, walking over to me or passing me on the opposite sidewalk. It was never her; at least, that's what I prefer to think—on two occasions the woman that could have been her vanished without a trace, leaving me with an uncertainty that still disturbs my sleep.

Now I'm starting to understand: deep down, I was afraid that I would run into her and that her face, or what she said or didn't say, would reveal the deep and painful gulf between her thoughts and mine. But I'm tired of being alone in my fantasy, of forcing myself not to dream up different denouements for this story. I miscalculated my strength; I thought that following her around like this was something I would be able to do for a long time. That the pleasure of it would always, deep down, be greater than that of finding her. But I'm no longer convinced it's such a good solution, this way of being with her without being all the way with her, of having her almost in view and dropping everything else in order to put all my effort into maintaining just the right distance.

I don't know when it stopped seeming reasonable to me—and, under the circumstances, I'm well aware of the irony of the term—to think that things might always be like this. When it stopped being enough, this way of moving forward motionlessly, of feeling I am wending my way towards a denouement; of thinking that a denouement is surely nothing more than that, than creeping indefinitely towards a denouement.

I packed my suitcases with a foreboding of disaster quite distinct from that which had had me ready within minutes at the Reina Amalia. I set out for the station under the deluge and the reproving gaze of the balconies and the two doormen of the twin hotels.

It's true that I wasn't in the best of moods when I arrived here. But even in more favorable circumstances, I still would have found this city unpleasant. And I don't like the hotel, which opened just recently and spared no expense, either. It offers unheard-of gimmicks and rushes to satisfy needs you didn't know you had. And that's no small thing, considering I get an endless stream of catalogues in the mail and thought I was up to date with all the high-tech junk toted at the trade fairs every year. They must have seen the jet-lagged look left on my face by the overnight—they offered me a "post-flight treatment" in the subterranean "spa." It included an oxygen canister, electromagnetic massage, and some liquid-crystal video glasses with projections of relaxing images.

Both treatment and hotel cost an arm and a leg, so I won't be able to afford many days here out of my own pocket. And I won't be reviewing it for the paper. I don't feel up to writing anything apart from these notes, and I don't want to put anyone onto my scent. When the deadline for sending in my article passes, perhaps they'll give my neighboring columnist double his usual space. He'll like that, presumably, and I wouldn't put it past him to have been cradling the idea for years.

I was thinking of her when I chose it. Or thinking *like* her, actually. I don't know if she'll like the hotel, but it certainly makes a good backdrop. This place looks like something off her website. It would be a beginner's error to mistake for cruelty the staff's impeccable bearing, the flawless foresight with which they anticipate one's wishes, and the distance—measured with extreme precision—that they establish before granting them. Really, it's the guests who demand this distance or who take it for granted. They pay good money for it, and they would be taken aback if it suddenly disappeared.

And I was lucky to find a room here. Someone had just canceled a reservation, and apparently all the beds in the city are taken. The winter season is already in full swing at the ski resorts in the area. There's gray frost on the windshields and ice in the tree beds lining the sidewalk. There's snow on the vast mountains that rise up over the city and that the train must have been crossing during the night while I looked through the windows into the darkness outside, a darkness so impenetrable that I couldn't be sure we weren't traveling through one long tunnel all night long.

After breakfast, I went out for a walk. At the door, hoards of guests were climbing into minibuses and cars. They were stuffed into fluorescent clothes that must have cost the same as several weeks' worth of anti–jet lag treatments. I soon came back to the hotel. It's the only feasible refuge in this ultimate paradise of winter sports. The city is everywhere advertising itself as such: there are specialist magazines on the newsstands, signs reading "Forfait," "Snowboard," and "The Black Diamond Run" over bars and clubs, offers on winter vacation packages at the travel agencies. There are cars with skis on the roof racks, shop windows showing off the latest in snow-ready fashions, and sunglasses that look like the LCD ones I was given at reception. They leave a mask of defiant white skin around the eyes of people's tanned faces. Everyone looks either recently arrived from or about to set out for the ski areas in the mountains. It's cold, and I keep finding myself one coat behind on this trip. A provisionary, chill breeze eddies along the streets as though we were standing offstage and none of this mattered much, as though the real action were taking place far off, up there, where the adults are having their fun.

At least the other cities seemed to be aware of my search effort. They played a part in it, even if it was only to make it more difficult. But I get the feeling that this one is refusing to even take the hint. Considering the results of my hunches thus far, that could be a good sign.

The hotel restaurant was deserted, and I sat in the lobby instead. I passed the time by watching the woman who was acting as hostess. She was efficiency incarnate. She maneuvered expertly, very seriously, and never inelegantly among the tables, offering tea and coffee. Her comings and goings, all her gestures, were impeccable, worthy of study; they were a reminder that there is an art to everything, a way of executing things properly. She wore a tailored suit whose only elements of uniform were the little brushstrokes of corporate colors on her belt and her shoes.

I noticed that after listening to the guests' orders it was she herself who disappeared and reappeared with a heavy tray that she would deposit on the low tables. I was surprised. Really, her role ought to have been heading up an army of waiters and waitresses to whom she could pass the orders.

I barely had to signal (not even a signal—I simply raised my eyes and met hers) to get her over to my armchair. The black coffee and newspapers I asked her for were only an excuse to see her from up close and to hear her voice. She smiled—just a little, but just right—and went off to the little bar in the corner of the room. I was surprised again to see that it was she who operated the espresso machine. And then she vanished, the task half done. The diligence of her wordless promise didn't seem to match the fifteen minutes it took her to reappear with a newspaper in her hand. No tray, no sash with the hotel's logo; she was clearly much more mortified than I was by this lack of formalities in an establishment that would appear to guarantee them to the guest as he arrives, and that doubtless charges dearly for them as he departs. And I think that the liking, or at least the fellow feeling, she inspired in me was mutual. That she noticed that I noticed the absence of these details, in the same way that one lost in an uncivilized country finally finds a person who speaks his language.

She apologized as she handed it to me—they could only get local papers today. As for the coffee, the machine had run out of cartridges and it would be a while before they could get more. I didn't have to ask why; my gesture of very slight surprise was enough to make her tell me that from midday onwards there would be some disruptions in the normal functioning of the hotel. It seems the parent company and the recently appointed director have failed to comply with what's been laid out in the industry agreements. Apparently, the unions have been nursing wounds and planning formal complaints for weeks. And today was the very day they had agreed on for a series of strikes and protests.

After a pause, she asked me with a pained, conspiratorial movement if I could hear anything. I remembered the man with the slippers in the poet's hotel, his inaudible radio stuck in a loop of repeated songs. Once again, I couldn't hear anything, and I told her as much.

"Exactly."

Her answer was quick, triumphant, and bitter. We ought to have been able to hear the ambient music programed to play twenty-four hours a day in the hotel's common areas.

She pointed to a used coffee cup on one of the little, low tables.

"You see this? Well, you shouldn't have to. It shouldn't be there."

But she can't cover the other staff members' absences on her own. In fact, she explained, she shouldn't be there, either. It isn't part of her purview as a middle manager. But today, apparently, a lot of managers like herself, and even some *directors* (she pronounced the italics), have had to get up out of their offices and get to work at reception or in the rooms. This didn't exactly mean she feared to get her hands dirty—though she must have taken her rings off for a bit, because I could see the marks on her magnificent fingers. The ones who drew the short straws had to make up the rooms or dry glasses in the kitchen. The head events organizer was serving the breakfast this morning. If they don't make progress on the negotiations, she told me solemnly, the hotel will find itself hurtling down the slippery slope from a discreet strike to an all-out war on strikebreakers.

She stopped herself just at that moment to look at the camouflaged door at one corner of the lobby. Two men in street clothes were sticking a flyer written in large, capital lettering onto it. We could read it from where we were. It was an ordinary piece of paper, printed in one of the standard fonts that come with any word processor. It had an almost handmade look to it, which was shocking in a place like this, where everything presented to the public is first submitted to a process of denaturalization and homogenization. As in haunted castles, the law here is that nothing of what hosts can see or touch must resemble what they can touch or have or consume daily, when at home.

The flyer announced strikes on behalf of the protesting hotel staff. It also warned that the contracting of temporary replacement staff contravened current labor statutes and would be immediately reported to the Ministry of Labor.

The other guests have started to get up. Without excusing herself, the woman, who was seeming more and more attractive to me but with whom I no longer felt the closeness I had at first, walked over to the men in plain clothes. Like artists on the eve of an opening, they stood at a distance to observe the effect of their freshly pinned flyer and to check it was straight. The three spoke in hushed tones before disappearing behind the camouflaged door.

I didn't particularly sympathize with the staff and their strikes. I didn't doubt the legitimacy of their demands or wish to deny them their rights. But I had gone too far with my own fight to start feeling solidarity with theirs now. If she was staying in this hotel, these disruptions might scare her away. They might force her to move to another one or, worse, to make last-minute changes to the itinerary I had memorized. And if that happened, I would lose track of her for good.

The impending strike; the hubbub and shouts that, without any piped-in music to cover them, could now be heard coming through the camouflaged door; the desertion of my precious few companions in the lobby—for the first time on this trip I felt abandoned and as though I were running out of rope.

And in view of what happened, it's lucky I wasn't able to rise to the occasion. I didn't know what to do, where to look for her. I saw no other choice than to redouble my waiting, ignore the bad omens, and forget all the disillusionments suffered after so many hours spent vainly in so many lobbies. To believe without faith and trust without hope that she would suddenly appear in that lobby, sitting at my table, as if by magic.

It seems to me now that, in a way, that's exactly what she did.

As I had done on my first night at the Imperial, I opened the newspaper in search of one last life raft. I gave myself over to the local press and its anesthesia of winter poetry competitions and cross-country ski marathons, its calming sinkholes and road shoulders and council members' bickering. I would have gladly drunk the coffee I had ordered, but I couldn't see anyone left who might bring it. I tried to forget the woman's lurking presence in the city, perhaps in the hotel itself, somewhere on the other side of the newspaper as I read it. She, who was doing who knew what or where, while I avoided looking up, hell-bent on reading every entry in the classified section.

LOVE. Get it back. Quick, reliable. Pay after.
TATIANA. Psychic since childhood. The truth, even if it hurts.
FEDORA Clinic. Abortions up to 22 weeks.
REQUIRED: Amateur boys/girls for videos & photos.

As I write this now, I'm surprised that I skipped the rest of the ad in the moment and kept reading. I was resolved to pretend that I had seen nothing, that I really was going to just keep on reading. But my tell-tale heart was beating so loudly that it felt like it would make the lobby walls shake. I think I looked around to buy a bit of time, with the excuse of checking that nobody had seen anything. Of course they hadn't. I knew full well that there was no one else in the lobby; that even if there had been, they wouldn't be watching me; and that even if they had been, even the most keen-sighted spy wouldn't have registered anything in my movements. I realized I was petrified. I put off rereading the ad for a moment longer. I stubbornly kept my eyes on the lines that followed, reading them one by one. For what seemed like an eternity, I played at baiting my angst— it was a good angst—and testing its limits, like a child postponing the moment when he'll pet the little animal being held captive in his room.

ENJOY *listening to me moan.*
HOUSEWIFE. *Will pay. Home alone. 18+.*

I read without taking in a thing. Much as I might put off admitting it for a few endless moments more, I knew I had finally found her. This ad was hers; it *was* her. I waited for one more second, until it hurt too much. And then, acutely aware that no one in the entire world suspected a thing or could follow me down this path, I slowly retraced my steps; I wandered back with my eyes along the tracks of small black lettering, pushed aside thickets of phone numbers and creepers of addresses, and found myself once again face to face—filled with a sense of Olympian magnanimity that seemed apt for this triumph of mine, and that I'm now rather ashamed of—with the ad.

REQUIRED: *Amateur boys/girls for videos & photos. Until the 5th of this month only. Young, presentable applicants only.*

A cellphone number followed. "Required" and "presentable" confirmed to me that it had to be her, as much as or more than the fact that the time frame coincided with the date posted on her site. Required. Who requires anyone to do anything nowadays? And who stipulates that their prospective employees must be "presentable"? Only she could have written that, as deft with the language of classified ads as she is with that of the photo captions on her website. I still can't tell if it isn't me who's adding in the irony I think I detect.

And there was that ugly repetition of the adverb "only", and the space-saving, tacky use of the slash. It had to be her. She must have been having bad luck in this city.

I didn't want any evidence of my cellphone to end up registered on hers, nor did I want to dial her number with mine blocked. I imagine she's used to being contacted by people whose caller IDs are withheld, but that kind of cowardice could give her a bad impression of me. I can now see, of course, how idiotic this was—as though my calling her at all, and the preceding pursuit of her that it would imply, wouldn't already give her the worst possible impression of me.

On the way to get my phone from my room, I had to dodge piles of sheets at the doors to some of the rooms, breakfast trays, lettuce leaves, lone shoes. Through an open door here and there, I could see unmade beds, rooms hastily abandoned. I passed a man in a tie carrying

162

an aerosol can in his hand. He avoided meeting my eye and said nothing by way of greeting, contravening the universal laws of hotel staff courtesy. His ominous silence was, however, the same one that reigned over all the hallways.

It was her. I recognized her voice in the curt hello she answered with, even though her voice sounded different on the other end of the phone from what I remembered. The telephone line seemed to have caught strike fever too, distorted as it was by buzzing sounds and vague murmurs. The hand I was holding the receiver with was trembling, and I had to lean my elbow on the bedside table. I swiped aside the old newspapers and the two recently emptied little bottles of whiskey from the minibar. I had hurried to dial the number after drinking them each down in one gulp, and now I regretted it—I was afraid of slurring my words, of finding my tongue suddenly cotton-like and clumsy.

For one absurd moment, I thought that the conversation would have been easier if I had tidied the table first. Luckily, even if it wasn't exactly easy, it certainly was quick. On hearing her voice I realized that I wasn't planning to tell her who I was. I would be able to explain myself better face to face; there was too much to tell her, and I was afraid she would hang up on me without a thought. I was relying on the faulty telephone line and on her not remembering my voice (and perhaps remembering me only very dimly) when I told her that I was interested in the ad and wanted to get an interview. She was succinct. She explained the matter to me in literally a few words—"erotic videos", she said—and forced me to lie when she asked how old I was. I was able to tell the truth, however, when admitting I had no experience in the field. I'm proud of how cunning I was on that account: I exaggerated my shyness as though I didn't know that that's actually a plus in her eyes.

There was a silence during which I tried not to think about anything. I read the front-page headline on one of the newspapers, over and over, without understanding a word of it. Just then, the sound of another telephone—a rabid ring of rude *Rs*—reverberated in both my ears at once: the one I was holding the receiver to, and the one that was free and open to the sounds in the room. I became disoriented, as though I were being confronted with the audio version of one of those optical illusions showing inextricable silhouettes that can't both be seen at the same time and that force the eye to choose between them. Then she spoke on the other end of the line, over—or rather, alongside—the sound of the ringing phone.

"Excuse me one second."

I understood suddenly, as though waking from a falling dream, that the ringing of the other phone came from both inside and outside the one I was holding. From outside my room, to be specific: the noise was coming, muffled by the ceiling, from the room directly above.

The double ringing stopped, and I heard her—now only through the receiver—answer the other call.

"Hello?"

Was she right above me, then? I couldn't rule out some telephonic coincidence, or an odd side effect of the two whiskies I'd drunk on an almost empty stomach. I gazed up at the ceiling like an idiot, as if my eyes could pass as easily as the sound of the ringing telephone had through the plasterboard and hidden concrete, the elaborate parquet and knotted rug which presumably lay between me and the soles of her shoes—maybe those same snakeskin sandals she had had on at the Imperial. I pictured her seated on the edge of the bed like me, a couple of yards above my head, one floor up, in an identical room.

She spoke briefly into the landline, without lowering her voice or bothering to cover the mic on her cellphone. A Morse burst of curt yeses and noes. I was thankful, really, for every second of that short conversation, which gave me time to regain my composure—although I have to say that the sensation of coming unstuck from the trusty surface of solid land was not wholly unpleasant. It occurs to me now that maybe the instant preceding panic never is; I'm reminded of the treacherous jab to the back of the knee with which my fellow columnist greeted me at the Imperial.

I searched my memory: I couldn't recall hearing any noise from the floor above me until now. None of the banging and stomping, furniture-dragging or marble-rolling that always end up making their way through from upstairs in hotels and houses (and that goes for the quietest and most sound-proofed, and even the uninhabited ones).

She finally thanked the person she was speaking to and hung up.

165

"Excuse me. Where were we?"

She didn't give me time to reply, but went straight on to suggest an appointment for the following day, after lunch, in a nearby café.

"Well, it's not exactly a café."

It also served food, and apparently, it's very well known. She told me the name assuming I'd have heard of it. But she didn't seem surprised when I told her I didn't know the place.

"OK, just ask. I don't know the address, but I'm sure you can find someone to tell you."

I was taken aback. Throughout this search, I'd never doubted that I would be the one going to see her. Out of a convoluted desire for symmetry or simply a habit picked up on the job, I had imagined our second meeting would take place in private, in another room at another hotel. I couldn't work up the courage to ask her where she was staying and find out if we really were neighbors again in this one. I agreed to everything and she promptly hung up, having managed not to be friendly for a moment.

Well, at least it was interesting, even thrilling, to hear how she spoke to her aspiring models. She behaved exactly as I'd imagined she would, in fact.

But that only occurs to me now. I didn't have time to think anything then, because the telephone in my room suddenly blared, making me jump. I picked up in full knowledge that it would be her voice on the other end of the line, handing down the summary judgment and the final sentence without any right of appeal.

But no—it was reception calling. A hurried, unprofessional voice confirmed that there was a strike and offered alternative lodging in a choice of different hotels. I declined, though they were plainly unhappy to be stuck with me, and hung up almost rudely. I wasn't going to lose sight of her now that she was, conceivably, so near. If anything, this phone call struck me at the time as proof that she really was up there, treading the floor above my head. It must have been they who interrupted our conversation earlier, to offer the same thing to her.

I inhaled deeply and thankfully—I realized I'd been holding my breath. Feeling light-headed, I tried to steady myself by double-checking the furniture, the not-yet-unmade bed, the street beyond the window. Everything was still in its place. That was something, but not enough to make me feel better. Yes, things were still in their place, but there seemed no way to transfer a little of my vertigo off onto them, to discard them like the old newspaper or empty bottles in this room and walk out without a backward glance. I felt these things leering at me, while the backdrop of cars and traffic lights ignored me like a man condemned. All a wild exaggeration, of course. But at that moment, the imminence of the make-or-break encounter hung over me fearfully, and more fearful yet were the hours I still had to get through in the meantime.

It hit me that I'd always relied on the idea of acting surprised when we finally met. But I'd pushed things, I'd cheated. The phone call had put me in a tight spot and there was no good way out. In the café, I'd have to own up to my lie. I wouldn't even have to speak—the minute she saw me in the doorway or waiting at a table, just exactly in the last place in the world I was supposed to be, the game would be up. Simply by seeing me there, all my crazy tricks, my schemes, my whole senseless quest would be exposed to her.

I had no way of knowing how far her sense of humor might stretch. Worse, I suspected it would only be all the more crushing if she took the whole thing as a joke.

As it turned out, I wasn't able to wait a moment longer to find out. Before I could think twice, I was calling the receptionists I'd just hung up on. They took forever to answer, and sounded pretty grumpy when they did. There were strange noises in the background: yelling and whistling and banging on pots and pans. I almost shouted my request to be put through to the room exactly above mine. I had to repeat it twice; first they didn't hear, then they didn't understand. They laughed. Then for the first time in all my years in the trade, a receptionist hung up on me.

I rushed out of my room and sprinted for the elevators, dodging the plates and cushions strewn along the hallway. I wasn't the first, either, judging by the broken crockery and coffee stains on the carpet and the baseboards. The elevators weren't working. Their little call lights blinked in distress and one of the automatic doors yawned rhythmically, opening and closing in front of the empty cabin. I didn't fall for the trap—I dashed up the emergency stairs two at a time. The sound of a chorus of throats bellowing out slogans in ragged unison rose up through the stairwell from below.

One floor up, however, all was quiet. It seemed to belong to a different hotel, one where the universal peace of collective bargaining reigned. A very solemn elderly couple stood motionless in front of the elevators, as if they didn't see the distressed flashing of the luminous panels, or were completely undistressed by it. There were no obstacles to negotiate in this hallway, and every door was shut. I walked along trying to calculate the approximate position of the room above mine. I arrived at a door exactly like the rest. The last digit of the number on the lintel matched. I didn't have the same luck as in the Imperial: this time there was no crack to spy through. When I finally raised my hand to knock, I had to resist the urge to beat down the door.

In fact, I produced a series of surprisingly decorous knocks. Rather like her own from the night she returned my visit. No sound from within. After a minute, I spoiled the effect with a fresh onslaught, a much louder and frankly boorish bout with both fists.

No response. The absolute silence disoriented me. Perhaps my room wasn't right under this one, after all. I seized on a last, wild resort. It seemed like a brilliant idea at the time, though now I can see it was the brainwave of one who has lost his head: I took out my cellphone, dialed the number from the ad, and waited to hear the ringtone behind the door. I even went so far as to press my ear to the wood. I didn't care how pitiful it would look if she did finally open up.

But nobody answered, and no telephone rang anywhere. Or rather, one must have been ringing in some inaudible or, in reality, unimaginable location: the place where she might be listening to it without picking up, at the center of a labyrinth through which no thread could guide me in this world of wireless telephony. The provider's automatic answering message kicked in, and I hung up. It seemed she would even deny me the consolation of hearing her recorded voice.

I went down the emergency stairs very slowly, one by one. The noise from the protests was still coming up from the lobby. I didn't run into anything or anyone on the way back to my room—the elderly couple weren't even posted in front of their elevator anymore.

I no longer have the energy to leave my room. To help me get through the night, I have to remind myself that all is not yet lost, that I'll see her tomorrow. It's odd how the prospect of our appointment can serve to torment or comfort me in equal measure. As dusk closed in, I looked out the window to see a long straggle of guests laden with luggage, a lumbering exodus of men and women, old people and children, trudging forth from the hotel. A sea of photographers and curious onlookers parted before them on the sidewalk. The staff on the picket lines didn't lift a finger to help; they brandished placards and chanted slogans. At first they had chanted a cappella (and at the tops of their voices). Now that an accompaniment of tambourines and friction drums has struck up, they sound a bit more festive.

I wonder how many of us guests are holding out, ensconced in our rooms. Around mid-afternoon, a few heads could be seen poking out of windows. By the time it grew cold enough that I had to close my window, I couldn't see anyone anymore. From the rooftop, to my right, a long banner with roughly painted words on it was hanging down. It was made of sheets sewn together, and they reminded me of the sheets, presumably meant to look like desert tents, on the lofty rooftop bar at the Imperial.

Writing kills the appetite and makes you cold. My feet are as frozen as the radiator over there. I've wrapped myself in the comforter to write these notes. It warms me up a bit, but it's no match for the forlornness of the cloudy breath I can see when I exhale. No good news from the outside world—just now a leaflet was pushed under my door, containing some badly-forced rhymes and a list of demands. Reasonable demands, perhaps, but practically illegible; the quality of the photocopy is as shaky as the grammar. I looked out into the hallway, but nobody was there. And nothing new about that dismal scene, either: the tangles of towels, the overturned trays, the wide-open doors.

I can fall back on the alcohol reserves in the minibar in order to avoid being starved into surrender, at least for the night. Fortunately, they haven't cut off the electricity or the water—which is freezing, but flowing. And I still have internet. If the worst comes to the worst, I can take refuge in the perpetually available rooms on her website.

Because I don't expect I'll be able to sleep; the musical reveling is going full throttle downstairs, and now I can hear giggles, and exclamations, and doors slamming, and running, and knocks on the doors across the hall. I've wedged a chair up against mine, just in case someone tries using one of those housekeeper's skeleton keys.

In the next room over, a TV is on full blast. Somebody on the floor below must be banging against the ceiling with a broom handle. But from the room above me, and from there alone, merging with the cold itself, falls a thick blanket of sepulchral silence.

I was woken up this morning by a rapping at the door. I'd dropped off in the early hours, rolled up in the comforter, head down on the desk in front of the lit-up computer. I was so groggy when I opened the door that it hadn't occurred to me that she herself might be coming to visit me.

And so I was spared a disappointment—or a relief—when I saw that it was a different woman standing there, the one who had served me yesterday in the hotel lobby. Violet shadows under shining eyes, energized and hoarse, she had recovered her rings and shed the company scarf. I was feeling my hangover from dining on the minibar stock, and it looked like she had a monumental one, too.

She either didn't recognize me or pretended not to. She announced brusquely on behalf of the management that the hotel was about to close. Any guests still occupying a room were kindly requested to leave the premises. She explained something about compensation and indemnity that I was in no mood to hear. I left her there talking, and when I came back out of the bathroom, she had gone.

I've stayed in many hotels at the paper's expense, but this was the first time I'd ever walked out of one without paying the bill. I couldn't have done it if I'd tried, actually—there was nobody attending the reception desks, and the employees, huddled in groups, ignored me as I went by. It was daytime by now, but it was still dusk in the lobby—the lights were off and there were large signs taped over the windows that looked out onto the street.

My first time without paying, and also the first theft of my life—I, who have never pilfered so much as an ashtray. As I was making my way out, the staff's indifference got to me; partly to prove that I hadn't become invisible, and also because I really was hungry, I turned back and walked into the breakfast room. It was empty. A couple of chairs had been propped up to keep the swinging doors to the kitchen open, allowing a view of surfaces piled with dirty dishes.

The dining room tables hadn't been cleared away and they were a mess of leftover food, crusty plates, and crumpled napkins. I sat down at an immense, round table set for a large group of diners. The cloth was mottled with wine. I helped myself to two spoonfuls of a fruit tart nobody had touched. It was floating like a desert island on a purple sea of melted ice cream, and I felt like a castaway.

At the back was the breakfast buffet, untouched and laid out in undisturbed perfection. But the burners under the metal chafing dishes weren't lit. Sausages and bacon lay crystallized under layers of fat, like insects in amber. The croissants had gone rubbery. My theft had perforce to be modest: I dropped a banana into my jacket pocket with no real intention of eating it. I forgot about it after that, and only just now, taking a seat in this café where we are to have our appointment, did I remember I still had it on me. Here it is, black and accusing, like a question mark sitting on the table.

It wasn't easy finding another room for tonight. We stragglers at the striking hotel—I was perhaps the last to surrender—had forfeited any right to logistical or psychological support from the absent reception staff. I trailed from one hotel to the next all morning, standards dropping along with the number of stars. It was noon by the time I found a vacancy in a cheap hotel, down a gloomy alley in the center of town. It was invisible at street level, but a sign was affixed to one of the balconies of the third floor it occupied.

They buzzed me in from upstairs without inquiry. There was no elevator, and the door on the landing stood open. You could see a tiny counter wedged into the corner of what must have been the entryway of a family apartment that had seen better days. This was reception, or rather a gesture towards one. An unsmiling old man received me. He seemed resigned to the futility of all the precautions taken to deter potential guests— now and then, some desperate traveler is still bound to uncover his lair.

"It doesn't have a bathroom. And it's supposed to be for four. But we'll just charge you for a double."

The room was huge and frigid. I paid up front and through the teeth. Sure enough, it contained four beds, one against each wall, around a big, empty space. Empty and useless; except for the absence of whatever item of furniture (of unimaginable name and shape) that might have occupied it, the whole space contained nothing but a gray sink dotted with cigarette burns, and a wardrobe that partially blocked the French windows leading to the balcony.

Peering into the little mirror over the sink, I thought my eyes looked baggy, but I was too restless to try to sleep. I came straight to the café we had arranged to meet at, even though it was much too early for our appointment. On the way out, I asked the attendant for directions. Then, without thinking, and for the first time on this trip, I dared to ask about her—who knows, she might have washed up in this place herself. The pictures on her website often feature rooms that seem just as bizarre, and almost as squalid, as the one I've been given here.

At close quarters, the receptionist didn't look quite so ancient. His creased shirt and flattened hair made me think that maybe he pops into the small room behind the counter for a snooze when there's nothing to do. Through the half-open door, I could see part of a calendar with Alpine cows on it. It was harrowingly bucolic—at some point, incredible as it may seem, the perpetual snows surrounding us must surely melt.

"About forty years old, dark hair, tall, attractive, nicely dressed?"

He let me speak without looking at me, perusing the stains on the wallpaper over my shoulder with an interest not yet entirely diluted by year after year of standing on the same spot. I was just about to repeat my inquiry when he spoke.

"No. A proper lady? Been a while since we laid eyes on anyone like that around here…"

All of a sudden, his eyes shifted to my face, and I was forced to drop mine. Only then did he redirect his attention to the damp wallpaper frieze.

"We used to."

The affirmation was made with such conviction that I suddenly became aware, as I looked at the relics around me, of a certain erstwhile prosperity ("glorious past" might be an overstatement), traces of that décor typical of the discreet hotel to which you could, forty years ago, have brought *a proper lady* without jeopardizing her good name or looking like a cheapskate.

I got the feeling that the flaking lacquered folding screen, now demoted to the back wall, was forever lost in reminiscence of those bygone days, as were the sliding door and, beyond it, the corner of the small parlor with its doilies crocheted many years ago by who knew what doughty matron.

She's not staying here, but I went down to the street feeling confident that she'd like the place.

I've had two cups of coffee already, nothing to eat and I have no appetite. It's pelting down outside, but it doesn't seem to even begin to melt the dirty snow on the sidewalk. The café really was just around the corner (like everything here, I find; the city is minuscule, though it seems enormous when you first arrive). Here I am, among tall tables and framed restaurant reviews that

179

don't include any by my competitor at the paper. I was going to write "neighbor", but at this point, I fear the term is inaccurate. So is "competitor", really; I was never much competition for him.

After lunchtime, the place filled up with old ladies of all kinds: alone and in bunches, demure and raucous, soigné and slovenly. It must be a classic for teatime treats. I am presently the only customer who is male and under the age of sixty. The aggregate murmur of their conversations rises and dozes off by turns.

Twenty minutes to go until our appointment. The waiter has taken the cups away and wiped off the tabletop with a flourish of his dishcloth. I thought it would be more presentable for her when she arrives. It seems this time I really am resolved to meet her.

I've tried to imagine what will happen. I've fortified myself against disappointment and tried to sound out the intensity of the relief I'd feel if she didn't show up. Maybe she's found other people to work with; maybe at the last minute she'll decide she can't be bothered interviewing a stranger.

Maybe she simply whirls right around when she sees me, without saying a word. Maybe she goes back out through the door the minute she comes in and disappears without even giving me a chance to explain. Really, I wouldn't be able to explain a thing to her.

Another reason I'm dwelling on all of this—I can't kid myself here—is to fake the serenity of a man who has abandoned all hope. I, who've always despised those who pretend to drop their desires while slyly continuing to keep track of them out of the corner of their eye. It's an old, cheap trick: affecting resignation in the face of the impossibility of something in order to make it come about faster.

I've stirred the coffee grounds. Unreadable, of course. It doesn't much matter; the future they might predict is very nearly the present. I've rolled and unrolled the little sugar packet between my fingers several times. I've placed it like a tiny bridge over a drop of water left by the waiter's cloth. A few minutes past the hour. I'll count to five, finish writing this sentence, look toward the door, and she'll be here.

She wasn't there. But in the entrance, closing his umbrella and glancing around, was the obnoxious man from the Imperial Hotel. The one who had kept out of sight while shutting the bedroom door, the one who was blowing into the eye of the boy seated on the edge of the bathtub, the one who had cast nasty looks at me from the bedroom door. She'd told me his name. On seeing me, the man arched his eyebrows in an expression of feigned surprise, screwed his lips into a twisted smile, and started to walk over to my table. Pedro, that's right, Pedro—his name is Pedro. How could I have forgotten old Pedro.

While he weaved toward me, I had time to recall the insolent "See you later" I'd tossed him as I left the hotel room. I even had time to improvise a similar mood. No secret oath of sincerity bound me to this man; I was under no obligation to tell him the truth, or even to make an effort to define it. I decided frantically: I would pretend I was there by chance, nothing to do with any appointment or phone call.

Good old Pedro would tell her all about it later, of course. I had time to picture that, as well. So much the better. Maybe she'd be tickled by the whole thing if she heard about it from a third party. It might put her on my side, it could establish a sort of mediated complicity between the two of us, in opposition to old Pedro.

"Hi."

He sat down at the table without asking. I nodded and tried to stop myself from looking sulky, like a child expecting to be told off. I didn't want to adopt the attitude he would have been expecting of me: that of someone who admits they're at fault. And so I grudgingly replied.

"Hello."

The man gazed at the ceiling and blew out a sigh before saying anything further. He looked tired.

"Look. She asked me to come here and tell you to stop acting like a fool. Tell him it's not like him at all, she said. Her words, verbatim."

The first thing to strike me was that "verbatim" too trivial not to be double edged. I couldn't stop myself blurting out a "She did?" that rather ruined my pretense of imperturbability.

"She did. She's got a damn good ear for voices. Even on the phone."

The waiter arrived, and old Pedro ordered a coffee and glanced inquiringly at me. I met his look with my own brows arched, mirroring his expression purely as a reflex.

"What will you have?"

He seemed nice, and genuinely tired. Not like someone about to say "Watch your back, sonny," or "Next time I'll break your legs," or whatever it is people whose job it is to keep snitches, peeping Toms, and weirdos in their place say. I wasn't sure whether this deference was something to be thankful for or an elaborately offensive way of rubbing salt in the wound.

The wound of having been found out by her. The certainty of deserving nothing better than old Pedro's weary benevolence.

"Nothing, thank you."

The waiter moved off. A new and still more exquisite wave of humiliation washed over me. She hadn't deigned to unmask me over the phone. She'd sent this guy instead.

"Even on the phone. Especially on the phone, in fact. She sees right through them, it's amazing. Practice, of course. Part of the job. You wouldn't believe some of the losers ..."

He seemed oblivious to the fact that I myself featured among those she had seen right through. That I was one of those "losers" he evoked with such uncomprehending compassion. Perhaps he wasn't meaning to be cruel. That's the impression I had then, and I still think so now.

I looked at him, feeling unable to say anything. And in fact, there was nothing really to say.

"So you'd do best to let it drop. That's what she says, that you'd do best to let it drop."

I couldn't marshal a single thought. Like on every one of the very few previous occasions when something awful has happened to me, a part of me couldn't help but be aware, at the same time, of the sheen of imbecility that these sorts of situations always have. So this was how it all turned out. Here was the denouement I had spent

185

all these months not daring to anticipate. I was about to cover my face with my hands. A gesture that's just another old trick: to make everything go away, to be the one who disappears.

What stopped me was the waiter returning. He set the cup on the table and poured in a splash of milk, raising and lowering the small pitcher with odious expertise. Old Pedro said nothing. Or not to me at least, because to the waiter he said, "Here's for the coffee," and handed him a few coins. Then he looked back at me.

"Best separately, don't you think?"

I couldn't drag my eyes off him. I found myself incapable of getting up and walking out.

"And go back to the writing, she says, she misses your column."

Another silence fell after that. Old Pedro took a sip of coffee, started, blew on the edge of the cup, brought it back to his lips, slurped briefly, brought it down to the table, and regarded me, eyebrows arched quizzically as before. He seemed to consider that some kind of response from me was due. And truthfully, I myself felt compelled to say something. Not for his sake—for mine. To utter some sound at the very least.

"Uh-huh."

Old Pedro weighed this up and decided it would do.

"And she's not wrong, either. I should know. Take it from me, I've been in this business long enough. Sure, it's got its rewards. Not just the money, mind you, though there's that too. You travel a lot. Yeah, it's worth it."

Old Pedro peered at me as though trying to read my response in my eyes, as though written across my forehead was the whole, all-encompassing, definitive tally of how worthwhile (or not) everything will have been when the final day of reckoning comes around.

"Still, it's tiring. To be honest, it wears you out in the end. Everything does. This does too. Wears you out."

He had picked up the banana absentmindedly, and was now softly banging it against the edge of the table. I think that's what I found more insufferable than anything. Neither of us spoke. He gave it one last bang, harder than before, and got to his feet.

"So there we are. I have to go. But I'm telling you: honestly, it's better if you just let it drop."

He was already on his way out. I watched him as he left. Suddenly, he turned around and retraced his steps back to the table.

"Umbrella."

I found myself smiling in response to the pally grin he threw me as he picked up the umbrella from the floor beside his chair. Some time later, I don't know how long, I realized I was still smiling into the void.

I was soaked through when I got back to the hotel just now. I roamed the streets for hours, with no sense of direction or time. The old man from this morning was not at his post. In his place was a young kid who looked like his grandson; the two shared a family resemblance, although this one was taller and his eyes were different, almost unpleasantly green. He held out the key before I'd told him my room number. The old man must have told him about me. Or I might be the hotel's sole guest, even though we're in high season. Perhaps I am the hotel's high season.

Another trait he shared with his probable grandfather was a knowing smile, a smile convinced that the most anodyne pronouncement conceals an infinity of meanings.

"Here you are. Room six."

I thanked him and headed for the hallway leading to my room. The boy spoke to my back without raising his voice, as if I were still standing in front of him.

"Excuse me."

I didn't turn around at once. In truth, I was tempted to pretend I hadn't heard. The boy addressed me again.

"Excuse me."

When I faced him, he had the smile on.

"My father told me that you're looking for a woman. Maybe I can help."

I felt my pulse quicken. That's how I knew that everything I'd been telling myself over and over again all those hours, through all those streets, was a lie. I hadn't given up at all. I thought: this kid knows her. He may even have posed for her, he's just her type. He'll be able to tell me where she is. Maybe she was already regretting not coming to see me. After all, she must be bored out of her skull with no other company than old Pedro. And her job was tiring, old Pedro had said so—it wears you out.

"Really?"

The boy grinned complacently at the eagerness in my voice.

"I think so."

"Do you know her?"

"I know lots of good-looking women. Many as you like. All you gotta do is choose."

I felt a sharp pang in the pit of my stomach.

"They can even go to your room."

I turned away. I didn't want him to see my scowl of sheer rage.

"No thanks. That's not what I'm after."

I took a few steps down the hallway. The kid piped up again.

"Is it boys you're after? I know some of those too."

I couldn't help turning round, already anticipating the smirk of innuendo he would be wearing. This time I forced myself to smile back.

"No, not boys either."

I got as far as the door to my room with no further remarks from him. I paused, my key in the lock. Once again, I mutinied against the idea of remaining this way forever, never knowing whether I had truly done all that I could. I've never known when to call it a day. I prefer to push on until circumstances themselves force me to stop. I went back to the desk. Funny to think how so recently, in the other cities, I'd been too embarrassed to ask the other receptionists about her.

"Actually, maybe I am."

The kid smiled at me. In fact, I don't think he'd stopped smiling.

"You bet."

We heard the front door open and we both turned to see the old man from this morning come in. Not all that old, apparently, since the kid who turns out to be his son can't be past his early twenties. The boy straightened his face and bent his head to study the only sheet of paper lying on the counter. He spoke to me through his teeth without looking up at me.

"I'll come up later and we'll talk."

I nodded, a gesture that also served to greet the old man as he shuffled up to the desk and returned my nod in silence.

I've sat down on the edge of one of the four beds to write. Here I am again, in a hotel, waiting for a visitor. I imagine she must have spoken to old Pedro by now. *Snitches and weirdos,* she had said. I hate to think that I've managed to insert myself into either category, or both at the same time. A peeping Tom, maybe. She said that, too. And she could be right. But I'm beginning to want to stop being one. I'm fed up with how action and company always slip through my fingers just when they come within reach.

When all is said and done, I think to myself, it was she who invited me to see what there was on her side of the door. I wonder if I'll be able to make her see that, by doing so, she shouldered a responsibility that it's high time she lived up to. She'll disagree, of course, and won't admit the slightest responsibility of any kind. I am curious, however, to see just how she'll wriggle out of it—and get rid of me, no doubt, in the same stroke.

The boy took his time coming up. I fell into a doze on the bed while I was waiting. When he knocked on the door, I woke with the feeling that it must be almost sunrise. I looked at my watch and found that twenty minutes had gone by. I sat up and beat at the bedspread to smooth it down.

"Yes?"

The door wasn't bolted, and the boy stepped inside with an admirable air of assurance; he touched a finger to his conspiratorial smile to request a silence that spared us any further standing on ceremony. He gave my shoulder a quick squeeze as he passed by my side, in a forced show of complicity that matched his smile. All highly annoying, really. He inspected the room, hands on his hips, as if he had never set foot in it before. Then he let himself fall onto one of the beds with a sigh of exaggerated tiredness and turned his perpetual smile on me once more.

"So, what's up, then, man?"

Clearly, he had no problem with ridiculous phrases. I didn't smile back. I was in a bad mood from being jolted awake. Asking him to come up began to seem like a stupid idea.

"How do you like the city?"

He didn't wait for an answer. He'd picked up on my distaste with the whole situation. If we carried on in this direction, it would be a slippery slope to ludicrousness. He jumped to his feet and adopted a serious, business-like expression and tone.

"Ok, you were saying you might be interested in a boy."

I played for time.

"Yes, but not just anyone."

The smile was back.

"'Course not, man, I don't know just anyone."

I tried to throw him off a bit.

"Actually, I'm thinking you'll do."

He had seen it coming and taken precautions: before I'd opened my mouth, he was already looking out the window. He didn't turn around when I said it. He started to laugh. It was hard to tell if there was any discomfort in that laugh.

Then he plumped back down on the bed, smiling.

"Oh yeah? What for?"

Now he was trying to make me feel uncomfortable. And I did feel uncomfortable. I did my best to reproduce his feline smile while taking a couple of steps across the room.

"Not for what you're thinking."

"And what d'you think I'm thinking?"

An exchange of this type—ambiguous and crass and liable to be drawn out indefinitely—suited him better than it did me.

"You think I want to pay to fuck you."

He looked at me, offended. Genuinely offended, but more by this violation of the tacit rules of the conversation, I'd say, than by the suggestion itself. He fixed his gaze on the bedspread and traced the outline of the floral pattern with his finger.

"And it's not for that?"

"No."

He stood up gravely, and put out his hand.

"Ok. Alright then, no problem, man. It's all good. I gotta go."

He didn't quite pull it off. Too brusque, too theatrical. Almost childish. We both noticed. He flushed, recognizing his slip as clearly as I did. But I knew—we both knew—that it wouldn't take him long to recover his footing. So I smiled and sat down on the rumpled bed.

"Wait. Sit down. I would pay you, though."

The boy's face did not relent, remaining hard and impenetrable. It could well be that that's his true face.

"I'd pay you, but not for sex. Sit down."

He complied. Not at all because he was essentially docile, and still less out of curiosity. Few people do anything out of mere curiosity at his age. Some learn curiosity over the years, but I doubt this kid will be one of them; he's more likely to grow old and die without ever knowing what it is. I rather envied him for that.

"I'll pay you if you help me find somebody. If you call her on the phone."

I paused before continuing. I had to choose my words with care. And then I didn't want to. Or didn't know how. All of a sudden, I was overwhelmed with tiredness, and with an almost sensual pleasure at the thought of giving in to it. Next thing I knew, I was spilling everything to this kid I didn't even know. The whole story, and I told it badly, too—not choosing my words at all, tripping over myself, skipping episodes, getting sidetracked. All out of order, in bursts, carried away by my own incontinence and how inappropriate the whole thing was.

The boy didn't interrupt, and I don't know how much attention he was paying; I avoided looking at him. It had been ages since I'd talked so much to anyone. I have now become conscious of something I only half noticed a while ago: it was a reenactment of what happened that first night in my room at the Imperial. One person talking too much and another listening to more than he needs to hear. Maybe she felt as much distaste for me that night as I had recently felt, deep down, for this kid. And yet perhaps she needed me as much as I did him. Perhaps, too, he felt that my confidences had abolished all possibility of trust between us. Perhaps he learned that night that certain outpourings will transform two passing acquaintances into irreversible strangers. Almost into adversaries, if not into enemies.

"That's where you come in. You could call her—she doesn't know you—you make an appointment and you tell me where. That's it. After that we'll see."

I corrected myself.

"I'll see, I mean. You wouldn't need to go."

I would go myself. Perhaps she'd be there, at long last. Or good old Pedro, of course. If I was careful, I would be able to shadow him to the place where she's hiding, or where I keep making myself believe she's hiding. The plan is as laborious and absurd as its own logic dictates. On the other hand, in its own strange way, it does have its rewards. Just like old Pedro said, and indeed just like everything lately.

The boy surveyed me, half smiling. He wasn't completely beyond discomfiture after all.

"Alright."

He stared down at the bedspread again, still smiling. We were silent. I had no more to say, and I waited for him to look up. When he did so, he had recovered his earlier smile, the one from the beginning. He was barricaded behind it as safely as he had been behind the reception desk.

"So how much do I get?"

I remembered what she'd said back at the Imperial. How involving money made things easier. I replied swiftly and without stopping to think—I, who am so hopeless at bargaining. I was surprised at how naturally I found the right response.

"Whatever she offers you."

He stared for a moment, and then laughed.

"Alright."

He dug into a pocket and produced his cellphone.

"Ok, give me the number."

He wasn't wasting any time, which put me on the back foot again. I have so lost the habit of consequences, it seems, that this fast-motion chain of causes and effects caught me off guard. It had been a long time since anything had ended up happening quite all the way.

"Isn't it a little late to call?"

The boy didn't look at his watch.

"No. And from what you've told me, it sounds like these guys work late."

I hesitated. He was right. Barely twenty minutes ago, I had been alone in this room and requested action and some company. And now I had the chance to find out how much I really wanted those things.

"So how about it."

It wasn't a question. I took out my own phone and read the number to him. The boy dialed and began speaking in a serious tone when the call was answered; his whole performance was surprisingly good. He didn't look at me while he was on the line; there were no winks of complicity or stifled giggles. Like me, but better, he affected shyness while answering questions that appeared to be the same as the ones I'd been asked. Before wrapping things up, though, he asked about the money. I feared this could ruin the deal; she might hang up on him or try to brush the question off. But they quickly reached an agreement and said goodbye after another minute. In the end, the whole conversation hadn't lasted more than three.

The boy fiddled with his phone for a moment, staring at the screen without saying a word, deftly raising the dose of what you could call dramatic tension. When he looked up, he was wearing a smile again.

"Piece of cake. Like you heard."

We both knew I hadn't.

"No, I didn't hear. What did she say?"

The smile expanded as he told me the amount she had offered. Perhaps I should have haggled. This is a kid, I imagine, who respects people who respect money. And the sum was pretty high. I got out my wallet, counted some bills, and handed them over. The boy took them without looking.

"Bit short, isn't it?"

I was about to say that I'd give him the rest if everything went according to plan. But I didn't get that far. I was sick in advance of haggling, and at the end of the day I don't care—I had to remind myself of this—whether I have this kid's respect or not. I gave him the remainder without comment and he pocketed it the same way.

"We arranged to meet in that café you told me about before. Tomorrow night at eight. It was a guy on the phone, I think he's the one who's going to show."

Maybe he was capable of curiosity, after all.

"I could go, and then tell you what happens."

"That won't be necessary."

"What, you don't trust me?"

"No, I don't."

The boy laughed again.

"Don't let it upset you. I don't even trust myself, at this stage."

He didn't seem particularly upset.

"How come?"

"Two hours ago I thought I was finished with this whole thing. Now look."

The boy answered quickly, almost before I had finished speaking.

"It's not too late. You can still catch the first plane tomorrow and be out of here."

I sat back down on the bed. Feeling exhausted, I decided to overlook his impertinent tone and pretend to take at face value what he had only really said to irritate me.

"True."

The boy took a few steps toward the door. I still can't tell if I'd have preferred him to stay. Now that the silence of the journey had been broken, the prospect of being left on my own again was harder to bear. But the boy was lingering. He eyed me from the center of the room.

"But you do trust her."

I could have asked him to leave. I could at least have protested, sworn blind that I didn't trust her, either, that she was actually the person I trusted least of all. He was right, though. You can trust this woman. Her website is deceitful and full of sneaky tricks; she lies, sure, but she stops short of making promises, or rather she only promises one thing: to provide—no, better than that, to sell for a reasonable price—a habitable space, four walls made and a roof over our heads. Not believing in promises doesn't mean we don't want to keep hearing them.

"Well, she's told the truth so far."

The boy came up to the bed where I was sitting. He stood still, and very close.

"The truth."

Smiling, he lifted his T-shirt with one hand. His abdomen was right at my eye level.

"Look, the truth."

He smiled.

"The only one there is."

I was silent, and it seemed for a moment that he had nothing to add, either. But something more always gets added. We always wait for the addendum, and it always arrives to find us ready and willing to hear it, to believe it, to repay it tenfold.

"And it's not such a bad one, either."

He picked up my hand and placed it on his abdomen, then a little higher, on his ribcage.

"You can touch it."

He released my hand slowly. And my hand stayed where it was. Under his skin beat the faint echo of another heart. We didn't speak, and I felt how my pulse merged with his.

The boy gazed intently into my face. I kept on looking straight ahead, at the contrast between his skin and the skin of my hand. Mine struck me as discolored, almost blurred, far less substantial than his. It's true they were beating in unison. But you couldn't trust that, either.

I leaned back. The boy retreated, too. His T-shirt once more hid his waist. He was laughing. Without contempt, I think, and certainly without spite.

"OK."

He sat down on the edge of the farthest bed and began untying the laces on his sneakers.

"I'll sleep here all the same. I'm supposed to have gone home, and my dad sleeps at reception and he wakes up easy. He better not catch me coming out of a guest's room at this time of night."

"Aren't there any other rooms free?"

"I didn't bring keys."

He had pulled off his pants and was getting into the bed.

"I'm gonna turn off the light, OK? I have to get up early tomorrow."

He half sat up, and reached his arm out for the switch. He paused in this position to regard me from across the room, smiling more broadly than ever. I suspected then, and still think, that that's the image I will retain years and years from now when I remember this conversation: the young man half reclined, wrapped in a sheet, one arm upstretched as if he were about to announce a tremendous piece of good news, some unexpected stroke of luck.

"You'll have to tell me how it all goes."

He switched off the light and we were in darkness. I heard him sigh a couple of times and turn over a few times under the covers until he got comfortable. My eyes soon grew used to the shadows. I'm writing, and everything stands out sharply in the orange glare of the streetlights. A peaceful rise and fall of breath is coming from the boy's bed. It's hard to believe, but it's true: he's dropped off. I've been smiling pointlessly into the dark for a while. It would seem that in the discomfiture stakes, I'm the last one standing.

I've taken off my shoes, but not my pants. My wallet, naturally, is safe in my back pocket. I can't decide whether the company of the boy in the far bed is a relief or not. It may well be that this is all I can look forward to, at this stage of the game, as far as potential company is concerned.

And anything is possible; incredible as it may sound, maybe something about this kid has rubbed off on me. Maybe I'll fall asleep as soon as I close this notebook and my head hits the pillow.

I spent the whole night with my eyes shut tight, buoyed on the breathing of my bed neighbor, trying to seduce sleep, to cajole it, like an exhibitionist whose wiles wouldn't fool the most gullible schoolgirl—feigning indifference, spying on its movements with sideways glances, waiting for it around corners, placing decoys and candies in its path, sweet thoughts that might lure it closer and induce it to open wide its arms and engulf me. Several times, I faked a declaration of defeat, to speed things up. Nothing worked. Only when I truly abandoned all hope and resigned myself sincerely to lying awake all night did I plummet into a dense, black, dreamless sleep.

I woke with a start and leaped out of bed. Without even checking the time, before assessing the strength of the daylight seeping through the still-drawn curtains, I knew I'd overslept and that it must be late. The boy's bed was empty. I stumbled around the wardrobe that obstructed the access to the balcony and pulled the curtain back. It was getting light. No, it was getting dark, and there was nothing but a grimy afterglow left in the sky. Just then, the streetlights came on, highlighting the cruel practical joke that I had begun to understand was being played on me. Their pale pink glow deepened to orange. I stared dumbfounded at them until they turned yellow. A joke, a prank; I had been swindled, robbed of the whole day. Never in my life, not even when I was fifteen years old, had I slept this late.

The bad news was confirmed when I saw the time. It was after seven thirty, barely twenty minutes before our appointment. I dived wildly at my suitcase, yanked on new clothes, and pounded down the hall to the shared bathroom. I washed my face while trying to calculate how long it would take to get to the café. I'd only just make it on foot, but I didn't dare risk trying for a taxi; I couldn't bear the idea of standing still on the curb, trusting to luck.

I passed the unmanned desk and charged out into the street. The pavement was slippery, and I kept almost falling over or knocking people down as I ran. I tried hard to blank out my mind, and before long it really was blank. By the time I got to the other side of the road from the café, I was ten minutes late. My mouth tasted of blood, my chest hurt, and my back was running with sweat under my coat. Through the windowpanes, I could see the old ladies sitting at the same tables as yesterday. A bored waiter was gnawing at his nails behind the bar. There was no sign of her, or of old Pedro.

I did suddenly spot the boy from the hotel, strolling out of the café while zipping up an enormous parka. He met my eyes for a second. Not in a shamefaced way, but not mockingly either; it was a friendly look, somehow, that suggested I should take things as they come and bow to the inevitable, like a good sport. He then got into a car that was double parked right outside the café. The windows were misted up on the driver's side, but as it pulled away I made out the profile of old Pedro, grimly set. Not with the grimness of a kidnapper or a gangster—more the generic solemnity that comes over people when they sit behind a wheel.

I wavered between screaming insults at the top of my voice, racing after them in futile pursuit, stamping my feet childishly, and breaking down in tears. Desperate to avoid the latter, without thinking, I jumped into the road with not one but both arms aloft, and almost got myself run over by an unoccupied taxi. I opened the door and flung myself into the back seat. I knew there was nothing for it but to utter the fateful phrase, the most preposterous phrase in the world, the phrase toward which, as I should have divined long before, my quest had been inexorably propelling me from the start.

"Follow that car, please."

The cabdriver chuckled, of course. Unsurprised, like someone hearing a stale joke that had once been funny (later he explained that it really was nothing unusual: not a week went by without him or a colleague being instructed to follow some car).

And follow he did, raising neither questions nor objections. We stuck close to our quarry's taillights through the downtown streets, jammed with traffic at that hour, abuzz with stores that were still open and with last-minute shoppers. We crawled from traffic light to traffic light until we left downtown and its bustle behind.

Everything slid in slow motion past the windows. People drive the way they are, and old Pedro drove deliberately and methodically, unimaginatively, without jumping a single yield sign.

The cabdriver soon grew bored with this dreary chase. He started reminiscing about similar cases, fortunately not angling for the details of my own. At first, I felt obligated to reply, as a matter of decency and also because I was terrified that he might simply up and decide he'd had enough and call the whole adventure off. As we approached the edge of town along ever-wider roads, we lapsed into silence. Once on the ring roads, the traffic thinned out; then, finally, we found ourselves on a deserted highway. It was easy to maintain the requisite distance from the other car, which continued to respect the letter and spirit of every article in the traffic code, signaling without fail every time it changed lanes.

Night had closed in completely. We cruised past residential suburbs, industrial parks, bars, and empty lots. With every white line the windshield swallowed up, the glow of the city lights grew fainter behind us. Markers slipped by on the right, keeping a monotonous tally of every mile put behind us. I began to count them in an attempt to blank out my thoughts, with relative success. At the thirty-two mark, the driver stopped the meter. When he spoke, it felt like the first human utterance there had been inside that car for centuries.

"City rates end here."

This sounded positively threatening.

"It's going to cost you a fortune."

"Don't worry, I've got plenty on me."

I tried to ingratiate myself with some jovial sociability. But I didn't sound very convincing, and the driver withdrew into an impregnable silence as somber as the night outside. I could feel his bad temper making the air inside the car unbreathable. I rolled the window down a little, then up again. Down and up, over and over, as we went several miles further into the increasingly solid darkness that hemmed the highway. By this point, there were hardly any houses or lights or anything at all to be seen beyond the ditch. I fastened my eyes on the taillights of the other car as if to magnetize them with my gaze and prevent them from vanishing into the murk without warning. Any moment now, on the basis of whatever flimsy excuse, the cabdriver was going to run out of patience.

And I thought that his chance for an excuse had arrived when old Pedro moved into the right-hand lane to take the exit marked by a sign a quarter mile ahead. I just had time to make out the icon of a skier over a superfluous caption reading "Ski Resorts." The cabdriver hesitated.

"So, what do we do here?"

Desperately, I talked him into continuing, while practically turning the wheel for him with my eyes, or so it felt. I had more than enough cash, this was a matter of life and death, and taxis were a public service—once the meter was ticking we were bound by contract, if we were to turn back now, I would regard the entire fare as null and void.

On hearing this about the fare, the driver gave a jerk and braked. I was afraid he was going to argue, or throw me out of his cab then and there, in the middle of the frontage road. I was sufficiently fired up to fight him in earnest, to wrest the wheel from him, to leave him on the roadside or lock him in the trunk. After a few seconds that seemed like an eternity—the other car was getting farther away, its taillights now miniscule—he stepped on the accelerator. The speedometer shot up, along with the fare, of which he intended to collect every cent.

We made up for lost ground. Now we were climbing a narrow, extremely winding road, with no traffic coming the other way and no signs of life on either side. The headlights illuminated the identical trunks of tall mountain spruce trees beyond the ditches.

A drizzle began to fall. The road was still headed uphill, and the stray patches of snow gradually merged into a single mantle that gave off a feeble phosphorescence. The continual bends—right, left, right—the steady swish of the wipers, the rain, and the intermittent red winks of the other car eventually made me feel drowsy.

The city with the cheap hotel—not to mention the ones before it, and what had happened to me in them—seemed very far away now. Even the woman I was chasing was becoming fragmented in my mind. This time, I really was sure that I was on my way to meet face to face with her, and it came home to me just how little I'd believed that until now. I tried to picture her face but couldn't. I started off well enough: I could see an oval form and some black hair, I could even sketch in eyebrows and nose. But the image kept derailing, and a different one would take its place— some strange, made-up face, or the faces of people I didn't care about in the least and hadn't thought about in years.

Far below, to my right, lay the miniature city—a sporadic sparkle behind the succession of tree trunks. As we rounded another bend, the tiny heap of trembling lights was swallowed up by darkness. I was happy to see them go. I wished, much as I had at the beginning of the journey, on my way to the Imperial, that this drive would never end, that the taxi would turn into a house where I could live forever. Stretching out my legs, I recalled the violent joy that would sometimes overwhelm me when I was little, in my bed, surveying the vast, virgin territory spread out around me beneath the sky of carefully tucked-in sheets. Perhaps, if it had been up to me, we would have driven on indefinitely.

But it wasn't up to me. The slope was leveling out; the bends were increasingly separated by straighter stretches; the trees were becoming fewer and farther between; and the snow layer had thickened, pulsating with a glow of its own under a sky devoid of moon or stars. We rounded one last corner. And just when it seemed we could climb no higher and we were floating above all the mountains in the world, the sharpest summit yet hove into view. On its slopes glittered a fabulous extraterrestrial city, like a human outpost in the craters of the Moon, or Jupiter, or those nameless planets so remote they make the Moon or Jupiter seem almost like a second home.

White lights studded the skyscrapers dispersed over the snow, orange lights marked the roads between them, yellow lights were the cars traveling up and down these roads, and blue lights ran along the cable cars and ski lifts strung up between the summit and the resort. Massive floodlights blasted the darkness off great swaths of mountainside over which myriad little figures glided—black against the snow, like tiny letters—moving downward in wide curves, converging and scattering, inching laboriously upward, swarming for no apparent reason at points whose interest was impossible to discern from this distance.

For the second time, I nearly forgot about the car we were tailing. Luckily, the cabdriver hadn't. Before we had got much nearer to the resort, he swerved right, onto a gravel road festooned with small, red lanterns. This road zigzagged steeply up again, causing the other car to vanish and reappear at every bend.

At the top, almost at the summit, loomed the giant hulk of a building that was much blacker than the coffee-colored sky. Close up, the forbidding air of a castle you go in and don't come out of was compounded with the industrial tenor of a cement works or a turbine hall. The cab driver spoke, mollified now that we had reached the end of the journey.

"Piolet Palace. Not strapped for cash, your friends."

I mustered some last vestiges of professional pride in order to reproach myself. The Piolet Palace. I'd been wanting to visit it for years and had almost done so several times. It was famous, comfortable, and dependably discreet, a model of its kind: the perfect place for her, and the perfect place for anyone who could afford it, really. I should have guessed. I made a vow never again to set foot in the Lilliputian town we had left behind. The vow was uncalled for, a mere rhetorical flourish—I knew very well I'd never go back.

The driveway led into an esplanade that had been swept clean of every last snowflake. Old Pedro's car, now empty, was parked between two other vehicles beneath a canopy to the right of the open space. The main hotel building spread its two wings like arms before us. The cabdriver turned off the engine. The ensuing silence drained me of all the inertia built up during the trip and left me feeling slightly dazed, vaguely embarrassed. When the man turned around to speak to me, I found it hard to pay attention to him.

"Here we are."

"Yes."

I handed over the expected fortune without a grumble and watched, as though in a dream, as the taxi maneuvered its way around before crunching away down the road the way we had come. Suddenly, I found myself alone and underdressed in the glacial night, standing at the entrance to this hotel like a sleepwalker coming to his senses miles away from his bed. Before I could decide anything, the opaque glass doors—embellished with two golden, intertwined Ps—did what doors in such places are expected to do. They swung open soundlessly, inviting me to step inside.

I walked into the African heat of a lobby that was even more silent than the night outside. To the right was a fireplace so large you could have fit the entire contents of a medium-sized living room inside. It flickered with the cinders of what must have been a terrific blaze.

Armchairs and sofas and coffee tables were grouped around it; some foreign newspapers were strewn about the tables, almost unreadable by the light of the embers and the two floor lamps in the corner. More light showed at the back of the room, where a wooden counter stood framed by two identical lamps at the foot of a grand staircase.

I approached with measured tread, noting how each step unsettled the eternal hush that enveloped every feature of that lobby. I kept expecting a cavernous voice from beyond the grave to reverberate beneath the stone vaults, demanding to know who dared disturb the slumber of centuries.

A small door set invisibly into the paneled wood behind the desk opened up, and a short man in a tie came forward with a smile.

"Good evening?"

The faultless professionalism of his greeting jogged me into action. I promptly decided to take a room, postponing my investigations for later. I wasn't going to inquire about her, or old Pedro, or the boy—even though they must have gone up to her room just minutes before. My arrival in the middle of the night, with no vehicle outside or suitcases in sight, was suspicious enough already.

Suspicious enough, in fact, for the receptionist to inform me courteously but crisply that the hotel was fully booked. He was an even finer professional than I'd thought—he didn't make the least attempt to sound sincere as he imparted his regrets, which of course made it all the more difficult for me to be confident that he was lying.

I was going to throw myself on his humanity, beseech him to give me the secret room that is always, always kept vacant in hotels like this even in the midst of catastrophe, even in the face of an avalanche of war refugees or massacre victims. That sprucely made-up room, invariably spotless, that bed with taut sheets permanently at the ready for the unexpected arrival of the exiled monarch, the disgraced millionaire, or the celebrity on the run: the various avatars that may be adopted in these establishments by the undercover messiah of hotel legend.

A thousand far-fetched pleas occurred to me, a thousand risible lies. I suppressed them, because I knew I wouldn't be able to hold back the frantic tone that would make me appear more suspect still.

And then, for the first time in all these years on the job, I resorted to the truth and gave my false name to the receptionist. I did this at the precise instant that the truth of my pseudonym—my sole truth—ceased to be one. I used my byline for the first time, knowing it would be the last.

The effect of this name, like a magical incantation, would not have been so fulminating in a lesser establishment. I recalled the hateful pair of rookie receptionists who had dealt with me at the Imperial. This man, by contrast, was truly an artist of the old school.

He handled it admirably. He did not blink, or ostentatiously compare my press credential photo with my face, or summon anybody else, or retreat behind the camouflaged door into the depths of his office. We were probably about the same age. Perhaps we'd spent the same number of years in the trade. Perhaps I'd spent as many years writing as he had preparing for my visit. Perhaps by the time these thoughts crossed my mind I was already losing it—because I caught myself making a mental note of his efficiency for a review I would never write.

"At once, sir. If you would be so kind as to sign the register, that will be all."

I signed without looking, like a statesman. The man made an apology now, and this time his regrets sounded sincere.

"Tomorrow we are expecting the arrival of a former president, you understand, and the entire floor has been set aside."

That seemed fair enough to me. You never get more than one night to solve a mystery in these places. Once registered, I tried to be pleasant, and perhaps I overdid it. I ended up getting carried away and even found myself, in order to really win him over, telling him the story about the receptionist at the Plaza who deadpanned, "Certainly, sir. Which of his several would that be?" to a journalist who'd asked for a line to the room where His Majesty was staying.

Maybe he'd heard that one before; in any event, he acknowledged it with a precise non-smile. After that, the formalities were minimal. In no time, I was equipped with the key to my room (attached to a miniature piolet, with the number inscribed on the handle) and the directions to get there, having declined the services of a bellhop to carry my non-existent bags. I ambled toward the elevator, happily reconciled at last with all those years of work and the long procession of furnished rooms and receptionists that had brought me here, to this hotel and this man in whom I had surely found an ally.

The elevator rose noiselessly to the ninth floor. The doors retracted to reveal a dimly lit hallway that stretched away to infinity, its far end lost in shadow. Although this looked unpromising, I hadn't altogether lost the sense that things were conspiring in my favor at last.

Or perhaps they weren't, or they were trying far too hard to do so. At first I thought there must be a large mirror at the end of the hallway, because I hadn't gone more than about fifteen feet in before I became aware of an approaching silhouette that, when I stopped, stopped too. But it wasn't a reflection. I saw the face in the glint of a wall lamp, and it was wearing a look of surprise—not the same as mine, I expect, but exactly the same as the one it had assumed in the café the day of the appointment. Good old Pedro.

He reacted faster than I did. He strode toward me mutely. And perhaps worst of all, he was smiling now. I took a couple of steps forward. Then I stood stock-still, as if my own immobility could check his advance.

And indeed he halted, a couple of yards away. It was an odd distance, neither far nor near, and plainly improper for holding a conversation. Perhaps it was a way of drawing an invisible line that I should watch I didn't cross.

He addressed me in the same tone as in the cafeteria: that of a man who had lost all capacity for surprise a long time ago. He seemed to be picking up at the exact point where we had left off before, as though we were still sitting at the same table, in the same city.

"The kid's already told us. He saw you getting into that cab."

He was still smiling, and his voice boomed in the empty hallway. But now it was his lack of formality that unnerved me.

"I told you before, it's not worth it."

The smile faded. The undertone of tiredness in his voice was the same as last time, too.

"What is it that you want?"

Besides the weariness, I thought I perceived a genuine interest, verging on solicitude. As though he were in a position to grant me whatever I asked, provided I was capable of asking. It infuriated me not to have an answer ready (and, in keeping with his sudden affability, perhaps even a sincere one). She had asked me the same question, of course, when this whole business began. Since then, I'd been all over the place without getting any nearer to an answer. I felt as stymied as I had that first night at the Imperial. Some people chase what they want, and others have to make do with chasing the answer to that question.

But now wasn't the time to go into all that. A pathetic impulse—probably the same one that had inspired me to hide, that first night at the Imperial—prompted me to make an about-face and go back into the elevator. I pressed L for the Lobby. The doors closed just as I turned to see old Pedro approaching at a leisurely pace, smiling once again.

The descent seemed interminable. Surrounding me was the uncaring hotel, and surrounding the hotel were the glacial night and the petrified snowfields of the summit. My pursuit had turned into flight, and all I had left was the animal reflex to seek haven in the human company and unreliable solidarity of the receptionist.

I emerged into the lobby in dread of seeing the man already there, waiting for me, magically materialized outside the elevator. I made it to the desk ten paces away, forcing myself not to break into a run.

Managing to return the receptionist's smile, I uttered an absurd "Good evening" that threatened to take us back to square one, to condemn us to repeat the entire ritual of the registration, the real name, and the vacant room.

He didn't seem surprised to see me.

"I was just preparing to call your room."

I must have stared at him like a lunatic, but he didn't bat an eye.

"I neglected to inquire whether you wished to meet with your colleague. He arrived yesterday."

It was then that I found my legs and the ground beneath my feet giving way—sure enough, my colleague from the paper, my section neighbor and probable usurper of my page, had just jabbed me in the back of the knee from his wheelchair, exactly as he had done days or months or centuries ago, with an identical blow that really did send me right back to square one and to the night of our encounter at the Imperial.

I spun around to face the same steely eyes, the same inexorable smile.

"Evening, neighbor."

I gathered from his tone that we could talk as much or as little as we liked, but that everything was already settled. That he wasn't about to drop any hints as to whether he had heard at the paper about my mysterious disappearance or been intrigued by the interruption of my column. He had never commented on my pieces to me; he may never have read them. He might not even miss them. Either way, he was going to chat to me exactly as if nothing had happened, as if we'd just seen each other the night before and had once more overlapped here by some coincidence of work. On top of this, he was going to act as if our encounters truly were frequent and habitual. And, to cap it all off, as if they were welcomed by us both.

I couldn't tell, though, whether he was taking this line out of shrewdness or out of self-absorption. Just as I had that night at the Imperial, I wondered if his bonhomie was a matter of calculation or of routine.

A bit of both, perhaps—they weren't mutually exclusive. They might be blended into some routine calculation, or some calculated routine, designed to alleviate the inevitable unpleasantness of living in the world.

The elevator doors closed behind us, and the gentle whirr of the ascending cabin could be heard. I couldn't bring myself to break the spell by withholding the reciprocation which my colleague's tyrannical good manners took for granted. More to the point, I hadn't a clue what else to do.

One part of me remained up there with old Pedro, who was waiting for the elevator and would shortly be coming down to where we were on the ground floor. It occurred to me that the food critic might actually be here on my account, as an emissary or spy sent to find out what I'd gotten myself into. When you're following someone, it's very easy to start feeling followed, yourself. I had spent so long looking at things through the woman's eyes, maybe I'd ended up letting someone else look through mine.

I returned his greeting as best I could and listened to his spiel with one eye on the progress of the little red light on the elevator panel. It ceased blinking for a few interminable seconds, then resumed, indicating that the doors had closed and it was on its way.

My colleague was here for one of his award ceremonies; he was heading the panel of judges for the famous gastronomic encounters the Piolet Palace had been organizing for thirty years. The competition was due to take place tomorrow, it seemed.

Although the receptionist had, discreetly, moved away from the desk, my colleague moved his chair to the middle of the lobby before continuing. I thought for a moment I'd been mistaken—that his initially casual reaction to seeing me there was a ploy and that now that my guard was down, he was going to spring questions about the reasons for my presence at the hotel, after all.

The elevator doors opened and old Pedro came into the lobby. In the time I'd had, I had sworn privately not to look at him. Needless to say, I glanced up and sought his eyes with mine at the exact moment his smile left his face.

The food critic glanced over as well, without interrupting his genial torrent, to which I was no longer listening. He looked at the man for the space of a second or much, much less, then back at me; but whatever he might have been reading in my eyes remained opaque to me in his.

Old Pedro, losing momentum or else redirecting it, banked to his right and drifted toward the low tables at the other end of the lobby. He took up a newspaper and remained standing while he flicked through it by the light of the dying embers. He was in the shadows again, reduced to an indistinct silhouette. It was hard to tell if he was looking at us.

My colleague talked on. But eschewing further explanations, he was now applying for my help.

"I was on my way to bed, but I've got to check the kitchens first."

He was acquainted with them already from previous visits, but during the welcome dinner the hotel manager announced that they had been re-outfitted prior to this year's contest. The manager had promised to show him around, but worrying news had arrived to prevent their tour: down in the city, apparently, a rash of catering-industry strikes had broken out and was now threatening to scale the slopes and infect the ski resorts. And this was an important award, a triennial Nobel Prize, practically, for restaurateurs. Tomorrow, the competing chefs would be arriving from all over the world, and they could be maddeningly persnickety people. He felt bound to make sure that everything was shipshape.

"I was going to get someone from the staff to help, but I'd be grateful if you could do it. With this chair, the occasional step or door can become an impassable barrier."

The timing was so heaven-sent, the proposition was so detailed, and it sounded so innocent that I assented nervously. I looked the man straight in the face and saw nothing but a frankness that was sufficiently unlike him to make me uneasy. And I'd never heard him refer to his paralysis as a handicap before. I'd never heard him mention it at all, in fact. As for the impassable barriers, that phrase rang a bell; I seem to remember it coming from some government-sponsored public awareness campaign.

Maybe the request for help was a veiled offer of the same. And elegantly contrived, at that: nobody's going to deny anything to a person with a disability. Here was a chance to escape from old Pedro in a way that would also spare the remnants of my much-battered dignity. I jumped at it.

"Let's go then."

He accepted my acceptance without ceremony. He didn't stretch his good manners—if that's what they were—so far as to thank me. He said nothing as he headed toward the farthest corner of the lobby, directly opposite where old Pedro was still hovering in the shadows with his newspaper. I followed the chair, not looking back; I didn't have to look to know that he was tracking us with his eyes. My colleague pushed open a hidden door in the wood paneling along the back wall. A sign beside it read: *No Entry. Authorized Personnel Only.*

"Not to worry. That's us."

As chairman of the judge's panel, he had been given carte blanche to go anywhere he pleased on the premises. I went in, hoping that the notice would prove an impassable barrier for old Pedro.

Beyond the door, it was goodbye to fine hardwood and soft luxury lighting. Neon tubes buzzed on the ceiling, and there was a massive freight elevator at the end of the whitewashed passageway. It wouldn't open until I inserted a special key my guide produced from his pocket.

"You see? It's a good thing you're here for this sort of thing."

I didn't reply. The lock wasn't that high, and he could have managed. I was reminded of the identical key it had been necessary to obtain in order to get up to the roof of the Imperial. Now it was facilitating a reverse journey. We were on Level 0; my guide pressed −3.

"OK, here we go."

Once more, the man was smiling with nothing but his lips, so I avoided his eyes as we went down. I didn't get the impression he was trying to catch mine, either; he sat in silence, staring absently at the doors. The big elevator took ages to go down. If it was going down—it went so slowly that the only sensation of progress came from the digital numbers on the panel. We eased downwards without a single jolt, accompanied by only the faintest of vibrations. When the automatic doors finally opened, they whipped aside like a magician's curtains, finally unveiling the box run through with swords.

My heart sank, as though the trick had failed. We stood before a passageway that was identical in every respect: same whitewashed walls, same neon lights. Here, though, their buzz was drowned out by a muffled, mechanical chugging that got louder as soon as the critic opened a door on the right. He had to shout to make himself heard.

"Let's cut through here to the kitchens."

We passed through the vast boiler room. It was brilliantly lit, a flat glare reflecting off the shiny housings along the walls. The very paucity of buttons and lights on them suggested that each one must be critically important. Obviously, pressing anything could have life-or-death consequences. Even a layman like myself—especially a layman like myself—was bound to feel alarmed at the potential for a devastating explosion.

This impression of imminent threat was not dispelled by the color scheme chosen for the machine casings. It was meant to be soothing, but the effect was as sinister as the malevolent throbbing it tried to conceal. The beige hiss, the ochre rattle, the hospital-green clicks of the mechanical hearts that kept the hotel alive—the two hundred radiators in the bedrooms far above, the water pumps, the emergency generators, the air-conditioning units. The place smelled of electricity, of metal and dust, of the black grease that oozed from some of the joints and gleamed ominously on the bolts poking like claws through the camouflage of the enameled exteriors. I thought back to the little hut that hid the softly whirring pulleys on the roof of my parents' building.

I took in all of this in passing as I hurried to keep up with my guide's wheelchair. The door out of the boiler room led, contrastingly, into a windowless box where someone had tried to create a habitable, almost cozy environment. It was furnished with sunken couches, wobbly tables, and rickety chairs that must have been salvaged from several successive eras of hotel décor. A banner wishing a happy 2001, some poisonous tinsel, games of chess, checkers, Parcheesi, and Chutes and Ladders—complete with shaker cups and dice—plus some Alpine waterfall posters; all this lent the whole scene the pitiful air of an attempt at domesticity. A brightly colored sign identified this as the Recreation Room. It smelled the same as the boiler room.

The critic swiveled around and we looked at each other.

"What do you think?"

I smiled lamely, to make up for my inability to find anything at all to say. He smiled, too, but not, I felt, with that edge of irony or superciliousness—and still less of mockery—that I would have expected of him and would have welcomed right then. He really seemed to be taking the room's failed attempts at homeliness seriously. Anyone would think it had been he, rather than some director of human resources or employee of the month, who had been in charge of furnishing the space. And now his smile was suddenly pensive, as though this desolate room truly condensed all the debacles of the world, as though we stood at the very epicenter from which all earthly desolations spring.

It brought home to me, not for the first time, how surprising the things that jokers take seriously are. And how inopportune, too.

"I suppose this room must be a real incentive to productivity."

I said it in a clumsy bid to imitate the jocularity at which he so excelled. He didn't raise his head or stop smiling. Instead, a moment later his smile grew even broader and took on a markedly different quality. Although he wasn't looking at me, I caught sight of the old, ruthless glint in his eye. I was a lot more comfortable with that, and I guess he was, too.

"Yeah. What a place for playing Parcheesi."

He wheeled up to the Parcheesi table, where a board lay with some tokens marking a half-finished game. He picked up a dice cup and shook it thoroughly, not very hard, as if counting, one by one, the number of wrist-flicks it would take to produce the desired score.

"Or Chutes and Ladders. As if board games weren't miserable enough all by themselves."

At length, he rolled the die onto the Parcheesi board. I stepped forward to see the result.

He peered at it, noticed me doing the same, and chuckled.

"But there's still something about them, isn't there? You can't stand them, and you never feel like playing. Until you start. Six."

He called the six at the same time as he pushed a token along, as one does in Parcheesi, even though I could see the number myself. He called it not gaily but with conviction, as if determined to go through every step of a ritual whose very pointlessness made it just and necessary.

"And then it's impossible not to take it seriously. Soon you're keeping score and moving pieces around and crossing bridges and going to jail, or back to Go. My roll again."

He calmly collected the die and shook again. His gaze did not move from the board as he rolled.

"That's your predicament, if I'm not mistaken. No, don't tell me anything. Each of us has our own game here."

And then he did look at me, beaming, with a flash of genuine triumph. At having wrong-footed me, I believe, as well as at the number on the die.

"Six again."

He held out the shaker.

"Go on, you try. See how your luck is faring."

I took it, to humor him, and gave it a shake. To humor him, yes—but also, let's face it, with the mechanical excitement that the childhood sound of dice rattling in a little plastic cup never fails to arouse.

I rolled much harder than I meant to. The die somersaulted across the board, jumped to the ground, and disappeared under a sagging sofa.

My immediate instinct, I admit, was to crouch down to get it. I had a fleeting image of myself on hands and knees, arm shoved up to the shoulder in the black gap under the sofa. Our eyes met and he laughed first, as if he had read the intention on my face.

"Well, I guess we'll never know."

He spun his chair around and trundled toward the door at the other side of the room. I followed in silence, automatically; provided it led away from the elevator and the lobby where we had left old Pedro, any direction was fine by me at that point. More than fine, even: the only possible way.

"Just as well, I suppose."

He spoke thoughtfully, without turning around in his chair, almost as though musing to himself. I didn't understand what he meant and didn't want to give him the satisfaction of asking. Nevertheless, he rotated slightly to show me his half smile.

"Another six from me and you'd have been packing for square one."

I followed him through the warren that branched out on the other side of the Recreation Room, holding on to the back of the wheelchair. We were entering a duplicate hotel, deserted and secret, buried beneath the other. On either side of the hallway, there were rooms with bunk beds for the on-call staff and a small employee dining room with plastic tables and chairs. There were offices with sclerotic plants, bell panels with switches connected to each of the rooms upstairs, cork noticeboards with timetables and snapshots of long-gone parties. Inside a dressing room with decaying lockers, a solitary shirt hung from a hook. Multi-tiered carts, taller than me, were stowed against the walls. At times we had to squeeze past sideways. Some of them held used breakfast and lunch trays, soiled napkins, timbales and rusty cutlery that resembled the chattels of a king who had been buried with all his retinue and belongings.

The rooms were empty and the lights were on. But all the light bulbs in the world could not have banished that funereal atmosphere. The air smelled musty and stale. The relentless throbbing of the boiler room reverberated in my throat.

At last we reached the kitchens, installed in a vast space with chrome-covered floors and walls. The industrial cooking ranges were fitted into metal countertops. Close up, you could see that the surfaces were crisscrossed all over with knife marks, like the lines on the palm of a giant hand. The knives themselves, ordered by size and type, were suspended in their hundreds from the magnetic strip that ran all around the room at shoulder height.

These knives were also the only recognizable utensil, and indeed the only feature that identified the place as a kitchen—no other tools or appliances were visible. They were probably hidden behind the metal doors of the storage cupboards at the back, and were bound, one felt, to have unwieldy handles and impossible functions. This inimical kitchen, which looked more like an operating theatre or the control room of an alien ship, made the concept of ordinary, harmless pots and pans seem foolish and endearing.

My guide gave a sigh of satisfaction.

"Ah, very nice, very nice."

He seemed to have forgotten all about me now as he wandered among the parallel rows of solid, metal pedestals that occupied the middle of the room. They rose as high as my chest, hiding him and his chair from view as he passed behind them. Lamps with huge bulbs hung down from the ceiling, so low they almost touched the tabletops. Underneath each one sat a small stack of white plates.

"This is where the contestants will be working."

I think he deliberately misinterpreted my expression.

"The lamps help. That's how the dishes are kept warm until they're brought up to the dining room."

He had disappeared among the rectangular podiums again. His voice reached me, but I couldn't see him until he reemerged at the other end of the room and beckoned me toward one of the three big metal doors at the back. The round, glass portholes set into the center of each one accentuated the underwater feel of the whole place.

"Come over here, this is worth seeing."

He gestured for me to open the door. I looked inside and immediately felt a gust of icy, deathly air on my face that made it difficult to breathe.

"The best refrigeration chambers in the country."

His breath was a frozen mist, but for the first time, I observed a warm spark of enthusiasm in his eyes. We were in the secret storeroom of a tribe of giants—the shelves were packed with monumental milk cartons, mammoth bottles of oil, colossal jars of mayonnaise.

There were crates holding tons of carrots and cabbages, and blocks of butter and chocolate enough to build an edible Tower of Babel. From great hooks attached to the ceiling rails dangled the red-and-white-streaked carcasses of entire pieces of livestock, like prehistoric hunting trophies.

I was getting goose bumps, and not just because of the cold. The memory of old Pedro on my trail began to seem confused, or secondary. Any second now, like in the fairy tale, the legitimate masters of all this would arrive to claim what was rightfully theirs and punish us for snooping.

The critic was engrossed in fingering some enormous pomegranates that had split open. I retreated to the door and spoke to him from there.

"I'm going back upstairs, if you don't mind."

He was lifting a scarlet pomegranate seed as big as a grape to his lips, and he didn't raise his eyes. I don't know if he only affected not to hear me or if he really was too far away to catch my mumbling.

I turned and walked briskly through the kitchens, toward the exit. I could hear the squeak of his wheelchair behind me, and I wanted to leave before he could say anything.

But I was cut off before reaching the door. With perfect punctuality, obeying my fears to the letter, old Pedro and his imperturbable smile stepped between me and the door. We breathed heavily for a moment without speaking, face to face.

He was the first to recover from the surprise. Actually, I think he still wasn't in the least surprised.

I looked behind me and couldn't see the critic anywhere. The refrigeration chamber was open and empty; the hanging lamps shone more implacably than ever on the metal surfaces. A last spasm of misplaced dignity or demented politeness stopped me from saying anything. I found myself stepping backwards, keeping the other man in sight.

He stood motionless. I backed away as far as the entrance to the enormous freezer, once more feeling the icy draft on the back of my neck. I don't recall whether he was serious or smiling when he strode toward me. I was rooted to the spot. Instinctively, I raised an arm.

And through the fingers of my outstretched hand, barely a yard away, so that I could practically feel his breath on my face, I witnessed a strange, almost slapstick scene. I saw him stumble and lose his balance and take an almighty leap toward me, a flailing but not entirely graceless leap. The open corners of his jacket flapped as though helping to propel his flight, raining keys, coins, papers, and cigarettes in the air. Part of me cheered the precision, the unerring accuracy of that pirouette. I felt the delight of the child who discovers that sometimes, very occasionally, reality will try its hand at cartoon loops and ricochets.

I stepped sideways to dodge him. He didn't so much as brush against me. I only grasped how powerful a force was concealed in the inertia of that stumble that looked so comically fake when, after an eternal second of unsightly windmilling, old Pedro landed with a loud, painful-sounding crash on the floor of the refrigeration chamber.

He lay prone and pensive, then moved a tentative hand like a blind man making sure the way is clear before taking the next step. I imagined him to be as dumbfounded as I was. Then came the euphoria inevitably brought on by other people falling. I wanted to giggle; at least I felt I ought to want to.

I turned around and scanned the kitchen for the vanished critic. Behind the last metal plinth in the middle of the room, I spotted the wheelchair footrest sticking out, and two small, malformed feet, now slumped off their saddle and twisted to the right. The brake release clicked and the chair rolled forward until we could see each other's faces again. His had no doubt been illuminated by the most consummate of all his Mephistophelean smiles, but I only caught the final shadow of it. He used his hands to reposition his ankles, and when he finally looked at me, his expression was sober.

"Close the door."

He gave the order calmly, he seemed almost put out, as if it were hardly worth pointing out to me what the most practical course of action was.

There was no sound from inside the freezer. Old Pedro was slowly levering himself up, without grumbling. He still had his back to the kitchens. The door made no grumble, either, as it moved around its hinges. It was nearly four inches thick, but I found it surprisingly light. One soft push was all it took for it to settle into its frame with a tiny, almost ridiculous click. There was no handle on the inside. As closing scenes go, this one struck me as something of a letdown, a sign that reality was reverting to its usual, sensible ways and hastening to draw a veil over an unexpected pirouette it was already beginning to feel ashamed of.

Were it not for the contents of his pockets littered over the floor, nobody would have credited that it was only a moment since the looming figure of old Pedro had filled the whole kitchen. Beneath the unforgiving glare of the ceiling lights, among the small change and bits of folded paper, glinted the piolet-shaped key ring with a key attached to the handle.

The critic was looking at it, too. Our gazes met, but I couldn't detect the slightest shred of complicity in his eyes. Or even of curiosity, truth be told. When he spoke—and he spoke immediately—it wasn't to ask questions.

"That service elevator goes up to the rooms."

I scooped up the key from the floor and walked over to the elevator door embedded in the wall that was at a right angle to the line of refrigeration chambers. When I pressed the button, it opened meekly and without a sound. I stood still and waited for him to go in first.

I felt an urge to peek through the porthole into the chamber where old Pedro was. But it seemed a mean-spirited thing to do, and I didn't want my page neighbor to think badly of me. If I'd been alone, I might have gone ahead. I can't deny that I would have enjoyed trying out on old Pedro the expression that the boy from the cheap hotel had directed at me just before he got into the car: a look utterly without shame, but also without mockery; a friendly look, somehow, suggesting he take things as they come and bow to the inevitable, like a good sport.

Perhaps the very look, in fact, that old Pedro himself would have turned on me if he'd looked out just then from the other side of the door.

Entering the elevator, the critic laughed uproariously the way he does at newspaper dinners. It was not, I discovered again, an infectious laugh.

"Up we go, then? I believe everything is in order down here."

Luckily, he stopped cackling when the doors closed. We both became serious, and I checked old Pedro's key ring—the number inscribed on it was 906, and 9 was the last floor marked on the panel.

I hesitated before pressing any buttons, and he noticed. In the wake of our adventure, a kind of awkward intimacy was rapidly forming between us. Now that we had ceased to be anything of the sort, we were suddenly like a couple of real neighbors. The kind who hardly know each other and are thrown together in an elevator for a ride that goes on too long.

"I'm going to the second floor."

He broke the silence at last, in a perfect imitation of the neutral tone with which people say that sort of thing in elevators. I say "imitation" because I sneaked a glance at him sideways—again the way people tend to in elevators—and noted that although he looked serious, a last spark of merriment was still dancing in his eyes. It occurred to me that perhaps, once again, I was the only one experiencing this neighborly awkwardness.

Because he remained serious and seemingly abstracted until we reached his floor. We didn't speak. As he left, he bestowed a final rictus on me, identical to the one at the beginning of the journey: a smile on his lips alone, belied and even undone by his eyes. It appeared we were going to part in silence, but he swiveled around again, in the hallway.

"Well, clearly you're not here on the job. What a shame. I'd have loved to read the review on this one."

It was just like him to say goodbye like that, with an indirect or deliberately twisted confession. He wasn't going to say anything about what had happened in the underground hotel, and I knew that the only reason he had found it in him to acknowledge (obliquely, and for the first time) that he had read my work was because we wouldn't be seeing each other again.

He took great care, at any rate, not to see the smile on my face. Before the doors closed, he had already turned his back and was pushing off toward the shadows at the end of the hallway.

The elevator inched up to the ninth floor. And once again, I felt grateful for how interminable the journey was.

My mouth was dry, and I was furiously, ravenously thirsty. At the back of the cabin stood a smaller version of the tiered carts that crowded the passageway in the staff area, and it was similarly filled with trays of cleared-away breakfasts and dinners. I took two gulps of milk from a china jug with two intertwined, blue Ps on it. The mirror on the wall alerted me to a white moustache over my upper lip that I hurried to wipe off. This did something to mitigate how much older I appeared to myself in the lugubrious light of the elevator's single overhead bulb.

Apart from that, I looked the same as ever. Perhaps that should have surprised me even more. The elevator, steady but slow, arrived at the top floor and opened silently. I had to tear myself away from my reflection—outlined against the exact replica of the hallway that lay alluringly behind me—before I could leave the cabin. I walked slowly down the hushed passage toward the door at the very end, whose number matched the one on the key ring.

I paused for a moment, the key in the lock—I felt obliged to go through the formalities and also to sternly remind myself of how much would depend, as of that next moment, on my every movement, word, and gesture. Then I rebelled against making such a solemn palaver of things, and I tossed my head like a docile child who for the first time refuses to submit to the cologne-impregnated comb that heralds important occasions. I turned the key, pushed the door slightly ajar, and peered through the crack.

Standing in front of the still-made bed, the boy from the cheap hotel, half-naked, was undoing the buttons on her blouse. She was focused on the play of his fingers and remained motionless for him. Her right hand was on the back of his neck. Perhaps it wasn't quite touching, though, because I saw it trembled slightly.

I pushed the door open gently and walked all the way into the room. The boy looked at me and smiled. An angelic, limpid smile, without an iota of insinuation. He drew his fingers back from the last button, which remained half stuck in the buttonhole. She looked up and followed the direction of his eyes with her own.

All those hours spent picturing her and remembering her voice had, it seemed, had an effect. She was prettier and she seemed more youthful, as if my constant remembering had faded her image in my mind. The change was plain to see, and yet difficult to explain. I was already searching for the right words and storing them away for later, for now.

I recalled the permanent guest in the room of the forgotten poet. It amused me to think that I, too, might give rise to the birth and dissemination of a minor mystery on the scale of my own little milieu, an intriguing rumor to be passed around after dinner at conferences or in hotel lobbies: the story of the errant critic who disappeared one fine day in the middle of one of his trips.

I took a step forward, and she made a sudden move of alarm or warning. She was looking at something behind me. I turned. In the corner stood—what else— the tripod and the camera. A light was blinking. I had just walked into the shot, and now I was in the movie.

I completed this novel during a residency at the Santa Maddalena Foundation in Tuscany. I am grateful to Beatrice Monti della Corte for her ever generous hospitality.

ABOUT THE AUTHOR

JAVIER MONTES won the José María de Pereda Award for his first novel, *Los penúltimos* (Pre-Textos, 2008), which he followed with *Segunda parte* (Pre-Textos, 2010), and *La vida de hotel* (Anagrama, 2012). Along with Andrés Barba he won the Anagrama de Ensayo Award for *La Ceremonia del Porno* (Porn Ceremony), and also co-edited and participated in *After Henry James,* a collection of novellas based on James' notebooks (451 Editores, 2009). In 2010, Granta included him on their issue *The Best of Young Spanish-Language Novelists* and his stories have appeared in numerous collections including *Puros Cuentos* (Letras Libres, 2011) and *Life in Cities. An Anthology of European Contemporary Writers* (Minumsa, Seoul, 2010). He is a regular contributor to publications including *ABC, El País, Letras Libres, Granta, Artnews, Revista de Occidente, Letra Internacional* and *Arquitectura Viva,* and has curated a number of exhibitions, including "Beckett Films" at the CAAC in 2011. Montes has translated works by Shakespeare, Dickens, Apollinaire, Mary Robison and Rachid O. and has also been a lecturer in Art History at the Spanish College in Malabo (Equatorial Guinea).

ABOUT THE TRANSLATORS

OLLIE BROCK has co-translated books by authors including Isabel Allende and Eduardo Halfon. His writing has appeared in the *Times Literary Supplement*, the *New Statesman*, *TIME* and the *Revista de Libros*. He has worked as a freelancer for the *London Review of Books*, on the staff of *Granta* magazine, and as a Translator-in-Residence at the Free Word Centre in London.

LORNA SCOTT FOX has translated several books from French and Spanish, most recently *Teresa, My Love*, by Julia Kristeva. Her articles and reviews in English have appeared in the *London Review of Books*, the *Times Literary Supplement*, and *The Nation*, and she has written for magazines in Mexico and Spain. She is currently an editor, journalist and translator based in London.

Lightning Source UK Ltd.
Milton Keynes UK
UKOW04f1800010515

250759UK00001B/1/P

9 788494 094866